CONCORD, VIRGINIA

A Southern Town in Eleven Stories

Peter Neofotis

ST. MARTIN'S PRESS

New York

These stories are works of fiction. All of the characters, organizations, and events portrayed in these stories are either products of the author's imagination or are used fictitiously.

 Printed in the United States of America.
For information, address St. Martin's Press, 175 Fifth Avenue, New York, N.Y. 10010.

www.stmartins.com

Library of Congress Cataloging-in-Publication Data

Neofotis, Peter.
Concord, Virginia : a Southern town in eleven stories / Peter Neofotis.—1st ed.
p. cm.
ISBN-13: 978-0-312-53737-1
ISBN-10: 0-312-53737-9
1. Cities and towns—Virginia—Fiction.
2. City and town life—Virginia—Fiction.
3. Southern States—Fiction. I. Title.
PS3614.E454C66 2009
813'.6—dc22

2008046215

First Edition: July 2009

10 9 8 7 6 5 4 3 2 1

For the teachers . . .

Numquam valedicamus

TOWNSPEOPLE

George MacJenkins, *a hunter*

Sammy Nolon, *a fisherman*

Jethro O'Pitcans, *an artist*

Betty Joe Lee deButt Carlisle, *an equestrienne*

Violet Graves, *a patriot*

Simon Donald, *an observer*

Tom Dorian, *a carpenter*

Mary Anne Randolph, *a loon*

Carson Falkland, *a voice*

Ms. Tzigane, *a Gypsy*

Elise MacJenkins, *a memory*

CONTENTS

CONTENTS

CHRONOLOGY

by Rachel Stetson

1951, Jethro finds relic

1957, Tom bound to the Natural Bridge

1958, The Church is abandoned

1962, Betty Joe shoots her dad, finally

1963, Vultures invade George's yard

1964, Sammy Nolon interview

1967, Silversmith proposes to Ms. Tzigane

1968, Trial of Simon Donald

1974, James Graves dies

1974, Mary Anne and Carson ride to the caves

1979, Elise and Alistair jump from Methuselah

Often I think of the beautiful town
 That is seated by the sea;
Often in thought I go up and down
The pleasant streets of that dear old town,
 And my youth comes back to me.
  And a verse of a Lapland song
  Is haunting my memory still:
  "A boy's will is the wind's will,
And the thoughts of youth are long, long thoughts."

—Longfellow, *My Lost Youth*

PROLOGUE

In Invitation

IN THE PLACES SET BETWEEN folds in the Earth, voices echo against mountains. This is especially true if it is blue-dusk; you are alone; and you laugh, cry, or call out for a friend.

Often no one hears your song, lost forever. Yet in a small town guarded by blue-limestone forested masses, a tale—like a ghost—can reverberate off the weathered hills.

The storyteller is perhaps a piano-playing townie who everyone thinks is crazy because she hears Indian whispers in autumn leaves; a reporter who has finished an article she was compelled to write, but now it fills her with shame; a mother who, despite the strongest of spirits, can never forgive the death of her boy. . . .

If the Muses smile on these echoes, these breaths will harmonize.

The voice sometimes watches from the stone outcrops at the top of Deadman Mountain. Other times, it sits next to you under a sprawling black walnut tree and shares a jar of moonshine as you both try to figure out what the heck is going on. Be it God or Gossip—the chorus sings of a particular community, in a certain valley.

It is we, the voices of Concord, Virginia—replenished by a mountain river—inviting you, friend, to swim in our abiding story.

I

The Vultures

THE MUSCLES IN GEORGE MACJENKINS'S face slackened and surrendered when he saw the vultures had moved into his yard.

He'd just returned with his twin daughters from a much-needed vacation in Duck, North Carolina, and he'd hoped to carry some of those sandy, sunny days back to Concord with him. But as he and his children, Mary Francis and Lee Anne, drove down the dead-end road that turned into their driveway, surrounded by a mature stand of white and Virginia pines, they entered a kingdom littered with large droppings, black gangly feathers, and piles of fleshy orange vomit.

They crept from their rusting blue Buick, down the flagstone walkway, toward their house. Mary Francis and Lee Anne cried out. The giant crows had defiled the girls' board-and-batten play-house, built by their daddy two summers ago, after their momma died. Excrement trickled down the roof. The birds had left the bones, hair, and entrails of their victuals dangling about the structure. They had even torn up the playhouse's rubber welcome mat.

As the MacJenkinses stepped onto their front porch, they shuddered at the blood trailed across their stairs and wondered what animal it had flowed from. They noticed the pecked-at caulking around many of their windows. The hose was shredded. Rotten vegetables from the family's garden littered the porch.

"Looks like they had a picnic," George said to his daughters as he gently kicked, with his bad leg, a watermelon, which the birds had somehow cracked open. Running his hands through his full dark-brown hair, he tried to laugh, but he couldn't.

Mr. George MacJenkins wanted to be a man of no guns. He used to be considered the best hunter around—and the second-best shot after Betty Joe Lee deButt Carlisle. But two years ago, he took his wife, Nancy, camping near the Vermillion Cliffs of Arizona. While there, they eyed a wondrous condor flying overhead. The large triangular white blades beneath the bird's dark wings marked the vulture as a gateway between this world and the next. Seeing the ultimate hunting prize, George took aim at the ghost vulture as it perched on the side of a nearby boulder and shot three times. One of the bullets ricocheted off the sandstone rock and hit Nancy in the lower belly.

He brought his wife back to Concord, Virginia, in a body bag. The condor, with its multicolored head, he'd buried on Arizona's Paria Plateau—he thought for good.

AFTER BEGGING FORGIVENESS FROM HIS two ten-year-old daughters, he locked up his guns in a mahogany cabinet in his basement. He vowed to his dead wife that he would not open the cabinet until he had sent their girls off to college. At that time, he felt he would be ready to take the next step and sell his weapons. Also, he imagined he'd need the money.

MR. GEORGE MACJENKINS WANTED TO be a man of no guns, yet there were black vultures in his yard. There were nearly a hundred of them, joking and jumping about in his trees like dark clowns, flashing their wings at him and his girls.

The summer the vultures arrived hosted other animal peculiarities. The day before George and his daughters came back from Duck, Old Lady MacJenkins—his grandmother, to whom he'd rarely spoken since his wife's death—was giving a walking tour of town. While she was bent over discussing the hand-fired glazed bricks that form our sidewalks, a big foamed-mouthed white dog emerged from an alleyway and bit her behind. She ran into Mr. Silversmith's jewelry shop and dropped her skirt. After putting on his reading glasses and taking a look, Mr. Silversmith immediately called the hospital. The bite looked pretty bad.

Later that day, Jethro O'Pitcans was leaving the Island Bar when the big white dog bit him, too. Luckily for Jethro, he already had gotten a rabies shot earlier that year when his pet groundhog, Chester, attacked him. So he didn't worry too much about the bite.

THE VULTURES PERCHED IN THE pines in the MacJenkinses' front yard, their camp the shape of a crescent moon. George and his daughters spent several days dutifully cleaning up the grounds. The birds, realizing they were living in occupied territory, confined themselves to the thicket of trees, as if it were a giant dormitory. From limb to limb they hobbled, keeping an eye on their human entertainment below. They had chosen George's home as a breeding ground when he was gone. Now that he was back, it was too late to leave. Eggs were already laid, so the birds would fight to stay.

A day after he had finished cleaning his front yard, George was on his way to work when he saw the vultures in the air. They appeared to have stark, white human hands on the ends of their big black wings. Flying in a large circle, they were searching out a scent while slowly spiraling downward. They looked like the flakes in the glass snow globes Nancy had collected. George kept the collection out even when it wasn't Christmastime. Often, he'd grab one globe, twirl it, and look into the crystal-held water's inverted reflections in the way he imagined the town Gypsy—Ms. Tzigane—might do. In them, he'd search for a sign from his wife. Now, someone had twirled his own snow globe world. But instead of snow, God had filled his microcosm with black open-winged buzzards. The birds spiraled down over his log house, landed awkwardly on the ground, and bumped into each other as they tripped in the grass. Like youths at a pool party, they hopped about and wrestled with one another.

When George left his house the next day, he noticed a dead deer lying on the side of the road. The vultures were feeding on it.

After working all day at his hardware store, he went by and saw Sammy, owner of the ammunition-produce-alcohol-fireworks-and-live-bait shop outside town.

"How was Duck?" Sammy asked when George entered.

"You got anything to rid one of vultures?"

"How many you got?"

"Nearly a hundred."

"You sure that many? You ain't going crazy on me, now, are you?" Sammy had saved George from going nuts while they were in Korea together.

"You can come by and count them if you'd like."

"Must be black."

"Yep."

Sammy laughed. "The only ones that will kill. Last year, a flock went after a couple of Alistair's sick cows. I got a few things in the back. But if Sheriff Wineland asks, you didn't get them from me."

THAT NIGHT, MORE THAN ONE hundred dollars poorer yet with enough fireworks to blow the ass off a fat man, George told his daughters to watch from the living room as he set up, under the pines, a line of Forbidden Roman Candles, Patriot Fourth-of-July Rockets, and Plasma Golden Fountains. He fired them off one right after the other, sending a wave of bursting, burning glitter into the summer welkin. The waking vultures took off from the trees and flew high, so high into the night sky. Rockets exploding beneath them, the soaring dark buzzards circled the widower, George MacJenkins, who felt his world twirling. He had to admit, though: the birds and manganese sparkles whirling around him were enchanting.

THE MOMENT REMINDED HIM OF years before, when he and Nancy were first married, and they'd spent the Fourth of July at Virginia's Mountain Lake. At dusk, he followed his naked wife into the water, where they playfully wrestled and splashed. As night fell, the lake's only hotel, on the other side on the shore, set off a grand fireworks display of red, blue, and silver. The dark lake smiled with reflections. Holding hands, he and Nancy floated on their backs as peaceful fire painted and repainted the air, water, and their skin. The surrounding woods came alive. Applauding his and Nancy's night swimming, the whippoorwills, katydids, cicadas, screech owls, and bullfrogs sang louder and louder, overwhelming the entire night, even the fireworks, with their clamor.

His pyrotechnics, though, did not drive off the vultures. The next morning, after George woke and tiptoed outside, he heard them sending their weak hissing sounds to each other as they hopped in the pines. Much of their puke, from the night before, was spewed around the yard, house, and driveway. He considered himself lucky that none had hit him. Looking at them happily move about their pine thicket, one could believe the vultures were rising after a night of drunken revelry. Partly hungover, partly humiliated, partly empowered, they tiptoed gingerly from pine to pine, nicking each other with their claws and beaks as they gossiped about their "night before."

"Those birds thought I was throwing them a party," George announced that afternoon when he saw Sammy the Snake Man.

"Shoot a few of them. It's illegal. But if you shoot one of them, the sight will drive off the whole herd."

"I HEAR YOU HAVE SOME black vultures in your yard," Ms. Tzigane stated when she ran into George later that day on Jefferson Street. She steadily stared, smiled, and then danced away.

The next afternoon, tired and feeling beaten up by some strange force of fate, George, in his work coveralls, sat beside his mahogany gun cabinet. There, in his moist one-bulb-lit basement, he thought about his wife.

GEORGE MET HIS WIFE IN eleventh grade. Everyone thought Nancy, who possessed her mother's Monocan Indian cheekbones and eyes, was beautiful. But people were scared of her. Her dark eyes held reflections in them, like smoky divining crystals. He wanted to hold her hand. One day, he summoned the courage to ask her if she'd like to go to a movie.

They first made love to each other the following summer, on a large red-and-blue-checkered wool blanket in the short-grassed foothills of Deadman Mountain. A thunderstorm—dark, warm, thick, and fast—filled the air with a power that swept over the deciduous forest and them. Swimming in the rain and each other's arms, they laughed as they wished they could hold summer, warm rains, and their closeness forever. As he kissed her body, he wondered how it was possible for a woman to be soft, young, innocent, and motherly all at the same time; and he was not ashamed of his almost Oedipal desire for her. Her long brilliantly black onyx hair spread like a shiny halo above them, and he rested his head on her bosom. As she held and caressed him in her arms, he wished she'd never stop.

Their daughters had their mother's high cheekbones and smoky dark eyes. They also shared her almost reckless need to swim in white waters. At times, George's heart stopped as he saw Nancy's image in the girls.

How should he honor his wife? he thought, sitting by the mahogany gun cabinet. *How could he keep his vow to her? Shouldn't he protect his children? He must,* he thought, *break his vow, take his gun, and kill the black vultures.*

He loaded his 8 mm Drilling. A daze fell over him, as if he were a young boy who did not want to be in school on a sunny September day. Then, snatching him out of his daze, he heard his daughters screaming. He closed the barrel. Armed, he ran upstairs and out the front door to shoot the birds. His daughters were squealing inside their board-and-batten playhouse. They were trying to keep the rabid, big white dog from getting in!

George raised his gun to shoot the animal. As he placed the beast within his sights, though, he realized the pellets had a chance of hitting the playhouse and harming one of his girls. He quickly put the gun down and ran off the porch, into the yard, where he picked up a stick and began wielding it at the furry werewolflike creature. He hit the crazed dog once smartly on the rump, causing blood to rise to the white fur. The dog whipped around, flashing its savage fangs at George, who then swung the stick again and whacked the beast's right shoulder. He moved to hit the dog again, but the dog jumped, grabbed the stick, then tore it from his hand. The creature dropped the pine branch below its paws and, ready for murder, looked at him.

George MacJenkins did not know what to do. If he made a dash, the wolf-dog would immediately attack him. Something told him he wouldn't fare much better if he stayed still. The beast stalked toward him in shrinking, crescent-moon formations. It stopped, stared at George, and prepared to lunge.

At this point, the oldest, rattiest of the black vultures swooped down and bit into the dog's bleeding derriere, taking off a hunk of it. The shocked, demented dog whirled around. As it did so, two more vultures dove, tore off pieces of its anus, and flew off. The beast turned to attack that couple, but as he did so, another vulture flew down and snipped off more of his rump. The crazed animal spun, chomping at the air, and then found itself encircled by calm, silent birds—all staring curiously at him.

The beast made a run for it, but right as he was about to breach the vulture circle, one of the birds flew up from behind and landed on its head. The creature yelled and bucked, but the vulture clung to its head and pecked at its eyes. The dog slammed over, onto his back, and the rest of the vultures, taking their cue, stormed into his throat, genitals, and stomach. Sticking their entire heads into the animal, they tore out its entrails. George jetted into the playhouse to join his daughters. And, through the small window, they watched as the birds silently yet frantically ripped apart the beast. Only the dog's screams were heard as the black storks methodically reduced it to a skeleton.

"HOW ARE YOUR BIRDS?" MS. Tzigane asked as she waited behind George and his daughters in the Red Front Grocery's checkout line.

"They have come to roost at my place a second year," he said, smiling and resting his hands on his girls' shoulders. "And we are happy to have them."

"You know, there are many legends surrounding the carrion crow, and how they were given the task of cleaning Earth. There is one from the earliest times, when the Sun wanted to live too close to Earth, making it hard for life to exist. Then, the vulture was the most spectacular of birds. Its head was covered with thousands upon thousands of feathers in every color. But the Earth was drying under Sun's rays. So one day, the vulture placed its head against the Sun and began flying away. With its great strength and wings, it pushed the Sun farther and farther from us. Though it felt its crown burning off forever, it did not stop until home—our home—was safe."

WHEN HE THINKS ABOUT THAT legend, George's mind wanders to that spring when he and Nancy journeyed to the Vermillion Cliffs of northern Arizona. He recollects the joy of that season, for he felt that he had married someone he loved with his all. "What more could a man want?" he asked aloud, smiling and rolling, exhausted, onto his strong back—after they'd made love by their campfire on the cliff's edge. The desert sky was more than crystal clear. It was so transparent there appeared to be nothing, not even an atmosphere, between Nancy, him, and space.

They fell asleep, snuggled in one large sleeping bag under a gazillion stars. Dawn, adorned in an amethyst-and-gold robe, awakened the violet-maroon desert. And a man awoke from sandy sleep, for what would be the last time, with his adventurous wife in his arms.

GEORGE MACJENKINS IS A MAN of no guns. The vultures fly down his dead-end road and roost in his yard every year, and he is waiting for them. To him, they recall that condor, with its ghost-like wings and multicolored head, which he shot in the Vermillion Cliffs so many years before. They echo thoughts of his Earth-spirited wife, whom he killed as well. They carry him back to the Southwest, with its close burning sun, big bright-beamed sky, sudden granite mountains, and layered sandstone cliffs. They also tie his heart closer to the ancient forested blue mountains of Virginia, which he unashamedly loves. Their large flock embodies the South's deciduous lushness, its temperate mountain waters, and its forgiveness.

Just the other day, George was sitting on his front porch when one of the black vultures awkwardly landed on his daughters' weathered playhouse. Urea trickled down its legs, cleaning them before staining the roof. As it shook off its feet, the bald stork's smoky eyes met George's. He saw his yesterday in the bird's gaze. He divined its curious hunger for the dying. Then he took a sip of his beer, nodded, and he thanked the vulture.

11

The Snake Man

"Woohoo! Sammy Nolon," Rachel Stetson summoned as she drove up to his place in her old Lincoln. Sammy was hurriedly putting his tackle box in his canoe.

"Ms. Stetson!" he replied, as if he'd been hit by a stun gun right before the words left his mouth.

"What are you doing?" she called out.

"I'm getting ready to go on a canoe ride."

"Why?"

"Because I'm going canoeing today."

"But we have an interview today."

"Ahh, Ms. Stetson, now is not a good time for me."

"Now, Sammy—you promised. A busload of boys was just drafted. I need your story for next week's paper. The AP said they might even take it."

"Ms. Stetson, I'm sorry, but I am having one of those Sundays. It's hot and the water looks mighty nice."

"Sammy—"

"Let's do it on a rainy day." He started to drag his canoe into the water.

Ms. Stetson thought about how it was August, and there hadn't been a fully rainy day in a month, just some afternoon showers. She put on her wide-brimmed straw hat, snatched up the spare paddle from the side of Sammy's shed, and ran to the riverbank. Stepping into his canoe right before he shoved off, she expertly steadied herself.

It was a peculiar, almost enchanting scene as Sammy's canoe moved down the Fork River, its forested banks chattering away with the mating calls of a million bugs. Sammy, big chested, with what look liked a hairy carpet stuck to his torso, paddled away. His grin revealed his missing left canine. Up front, Ms. Stetson, whom he'd been avoiding for weeks, sat in her calico dress. Her high heels rested beside her bare feet and Sammy's tackle box.

"A canoe ride. How delightful. It's been years. Since my journeys in Amazonia."

Down by Sammy's house, the Fork River is large and wide, with just a few rapids here and there, adding a soft white sound to the air. On the right was a high cliff of dark stone, which glowed in the three o'clock light. The water was clear and the color of dark amber.

"Now, Sammy, I'm going to record you." She pulled out her pens, pads, and recorder.

"Oh, I don't know. I'm not very articulate."

"I trust you'll do fine." She set up her Morton Smith.

Sammy looked around himself, worried.

"Now that our boys are going off to Vietnam, I want to talk with you about your experience in Korea."

"No one wants to hear me blab about that old war."

"Sure they do. Now come on. Why did you and George sign up? To stop the Reds?"

"Just to get out of town," he replied, paddling away. "I was working as a junk man. And George's grandmother was driving him crazy because he was dating that Indian."

She laughed. "And what was it like to get out of Concord, Virginia?"

"It was like being thrown into outer space. After basic training at Camp Rucker, Alabama, we took the troop train to California—where they shipped us off. In route, we encountered a two-day sea storm. George and I worked on board with hip boots. We were the only ones who didn't get seasick."

"Why didn't you?"

"I don't know," he said, paddling away. "We landed in Japan, where we loaded supplies to invade Inch'on. Then they tossed us onto a ship. In the middle of the night, they threw some ladder ropes overboard. I thought to myself, *Hail Mary, here we go.* You should have seen George's face when they handed him our M-1 Geralds; they were rusty versions of the same gun his uncle Jim had brought back from fighting Hitler."

"And what were those first few weeks of fighting like?"

"Hold on to the side of the boat now. We're going through some rapids."

The boat jostled, and Ms. Stetson grabbed the right side of the canoe.

"You mind helping me steer through this part? I'm afraid I'm not as agile as I used to be."

THE TWO COMRADES CAME TO a bend in the river. Here, the water was especially deep and narrow. On either side was a steep slope, packed with large Virginia and table mountain pines. Their shade, created by the slanted three-thirty sun, sheeted over the water of the floating voyagers.

"Why do you think George can't remember Korea?" Ms. Stetson asked.

"Who told you he can't remember?"

"He never talks about it."

"That don't mean nothing. Just 'cause you can't talk about shit doesn't mean it doesn't stink."

"According to his grandmother, he's suffered from complete amnesia. She says she's very grateful to you for looking after him—"

"I swear, that old lady, sh—" Sammy stopped himself short.

"What about her?" Ms. Stetson smirked.

"Loves to talk."

Sammy opened his cooler and popped a bottle of Pabst. He took a deep gulp and then set it on his thick hairy thigh.

"I don't know why George does anything that he does. You want a beer?"

"No, but thank you for asking."

"You know, he's been through a lot in his life, losing his parents and his wife. Maybe there is just not enough room in his mind for Korea."

Two dragonflies, scarlet-maroon, landed on her straw hat, yet she did not brush them away. "So, can you tell me what it was like once you entered combat?"

Careful not to look at Ms. Stetson, Sammy picked up his rod and reel and poked a black pork rind onto the line. "Mind if I do a little fishing?"

"Not at all. As I was saying, I think the boys heading off could benefit from any advice you might have related to your experience in Asia."

"Shhh—let's not make too much racket. I don't want to scare away the fish."

"Sammy, you can't expect me to keep my mouth shut for an entire—"

"Yeah, yeah. Hold on. Let me just make a few more casts." They waited a few moments.

"WHEN WERE YOU—?"

"Hey, look here, I got a bite already." Sammy laughed. He felt the line's pull. "That's funny," he said. He looked into the water. "Well, I'll be—" Sammy pulled up the line. "Look."

Glancing up from her notebook, Rachel saw a six-foot-long red snake shaking in the air. She recoiled. "Snap its spine, Sammy."

"Where's your camera, Ms. Stetson?"

"What?"

"Take a photo, lady!"

Trembling, Rachel fumbled open her camera case and prepared to shoot. Sammy grabbed the footless dragon by the neck. It wrangled in the air. The serpent flashed open its fangs, and Sammy quickly turned out the hook from the lower jaw.

"Well, at least he was able to swallow the pork rind," Sammy commented. The serpent hissed. Sammy turned the head to face Rachel and smiled. "Say cheese," he urged.

Sammy and the snake smiled. Ms. Stetson steadied herself and snapped the photo.

"Well, nice knowing you." He tossed the devil into the water.

"Sammy!"

"Yes."

"What the hell are you doing letting that serpent go?"

"Catch and release."

"What?"

"Are you ever up late enough to see those TV shows about alien abductions? Some dude in a cornfield gets sucked up by an extraterrestrial beam? The poor fellow can't try to escape because he's in outer nowhere. The wild-eyed guy then talks about being thrown back—defiled and naked—and no one believing him. I often see those shows and think to myself, 'Shoot, this guy must be nuts. Absolutely bonkers. But I believe him. Hell, it happened to me. Except, I bet aliens know what they're doing.' "

Rachel searched inside Sammy for the boy she used to babysit, decades ago. "Sammy, you mind if I do have that beer?"

"My pleasure." Light shined intermittently through the canopy of sycamore trees leaning over the water, sending jagged shadows over the boaters' faces.

"Once you were captured, how did you tough it out?"

"I don't know."

"Come on, Sammy. Think of Jimmy Graves going off—"

"Rachel, by the end, we looked like beat-up walking stick bugs. What do you want me to say?"

The river came to another bend. The wind blew, and Ms. Stetson took off her hat. She helped him paddle through a few rapids. Now near Pumpkin Rock, Sammy lassoed the boat to a large triangular stone jutting out of the water.

At Pumpkin Rock, the long narrow rapids fall into a deep pool, which curves around a series of large granite boulders, the largest, of course, being Pumpkin Rock, which stands about two stories out of the deep water. Its vast network of grooves begins to tell the story of its eons-old battle with the river. By providing easy climbing, they—unlike human scars—have assured its popularity in civilian life.

"How did you handle life in the prisoner camps?" She brought the tape recorder closer to Sammy.

"It's time for a dip." He leapt into the water. When he finally emerged, he shook his head like a shaggy dog and gasped with delight.

"You don't think there are more snakes cooling off today?" She perched over the side of the canoe and watched Sammy float on his back. "Seriously, Sammy, what happened over there? How did you and George survive?"

"Weed."

"Excuse me?"

"I'm serious. During the first spring, the Turks with us pointed out that marijuana grew freely around us. I started rolling George a joint every day and no longer had to force-feed him."

"The marijuana, then, brought back his spirit?"

"His appetite. When things got really bad, we'd grab bushels of the stuff and smoke it together. And there'd we be, laughing, hollering, hollow-faced, teeth falling out, lice everywhere, and having a good old time."

She placed her hand in the water and sprinkled it on her forehead.

"Why don't you get in?" he asked.

"Oh, I can't."

"Why not?"

"Well, for one thing, I didn't bring my bathing suit."

"Swim in your dress."

"Excuse me?"

"It's just water. It's not going to hurt anything."

"I don't think that is a good idea."

"Neither of us is getting any younger, and it sure is hot. Sometimes, you have to just jump into the water and swim."

Ms. Stetson looked at Sammy, floating on his back with his arms spread out, like a big, fat, hairy Jesus crucified or baptized.

She flopped into the water. The splash from her entrance shook Sammy from his position, and he laughed heartily as she rose to the surface. The bubbles in her calico dress made it float around her.

"Sammy, you're making me act like a girl again."

Sammy laughed, swam over to Pumpkin Rock, and climbed its side. One, two, three, his feet and hands went into the rock's grooves, letting him scale it.

"Be careful, now. I'm not strong enough to haul you out of this river with a broken limb." She dog-paddled gaily away from the canoe.

"I will be," he said, laughing as he reached the top. Once there, he raised his arms and roared.

Looking at him, Ms. Stetson laughed. She then glanced upstream. "Sammy, is that—?"

There, bobbing down the rapids, was that giant water snake, now with a mate.

"Sammy, Sammy, it's the snake! Oh, God no, there's two of them!"

Ms. Stetson looked ahead and around herself, not knowing how to escape. The serpents, each with its head above the water, were moving straight toward her and her calico dress.

"I can't get out of the water fast enough. The current—"

Ms. Stetson tried to move toward the riverbank. But she lost her footing and tumbled downstream into quicker current. She anchored herself right before the rapids after Pumpkin Rock's pool. Up to her breast in water, she glared upstream at the oncoming serpents.

"Sammy!" she wailed.

The seducers of Eve slithered straight toward the reporter. Their heads moved from side to side; their tongues flickered in the air.

"Rachel, look at me. Just look at me."

Rachel turned and looked, with desperation, up at the Snake Man.

"Stay still and keep looking at me."

Rachel Stetson froze. The river carried the serpents closer. When they were within feet of her neck, she shuddered.

"Stay still."

THEY PASSED HER, ONE ON either side, steady like a pair of race-horses. When their heads finally went by, Ms. Stetson let out her breath. She unlocked her eyes from Sammy's to catch the long slithering tails only inches from her neck. One tapped her gently on the shoulder. She swore she saw the snake look back and smirk.

Ms. Stetson stared up at Sammy, who was grinning.

"They're just migrating."

"I'm getting back into the boat, Sammy."

THE TRAVELERS DRIFTED IN SILENCE for some time, allowing the wind and sun to dry them off. The continual cries of the insects and the white noise of the distant rapids calmed her nerves.

"Your mother was a Pentecostal snake handler. I remember years ago, when Jethro found the fossil. My father commented that she'd even introduced you to the practice."

"She was a dangerous woman."

"So, is that how you survived over there? Surrounded by snakes, you just stayed still?" Purple boulders were on either side of them.

"Why do you keep on bringing this up?"

"Because it's important. You owe it to the next generation of soldiers. Everyone thinks they're just going on a coon hunt in Asia."

Sammy stopped paddling. Rachel turned in her seat to face him. "It has been quite a boat ride with you, Sammy. I deserve my story."

The wind picked up from downstream, carrying with it a strange, unnatural scent.

"All right, I'll give you a tale for the troops," he coldly stated.

"WE WERE SENT TO THE front lines on July ninth. I remember because it was George's grandma's birthday. We were told it was just going to be a pigeon shoot. When two of our companies were overrun, we moved to counterattack. We had about a hundred fifty men, and suddenly, over the hill, like a bunch of yellow jackets, swarmed five thousand North Koreans with T-34 Tanks. There we were, out of ammunition.

"After being dragged here and there for a few weeks, we were all forced to go on the ungodly march through the hills—to the camps where we'd be kept for the rest of the war. A Korean who called himself Tiger led the trail. As soldiers fell out, exhausted, they were shot by the NK troops. I saw one Tennessean hillbilly flop on his back and start making a snow angel. His towheaded friend begged him to get up, but he wouldn't, and a Korean soldier shot the snow angel–making man through the heart. I saw another boy, with a blood-filled mouth, fall onto his knees and start belting 'God Bless America' in a raspy, beautiful voice—one that even Carson Falkland would have been impressed by. He never got to finish the song. George had gotten some shrapnel in his calf when he was captured, and that gave him some problems—but I helped him along.

"This one night during the march, we were all forced to sleep in this rickety schoolhouse, all on top of each other, like a bunch of fish thrown into a waterless barrel. At first, we couldn't help but flip and flap around on top of each other, gasping for more air, but there was none. Eventually, we settled down as best we could. Then, in the middle of the night, a few kids started crying. They couldn't help it, I suppose. But the NK kept on screaming and shooting bullets into the roof—warning us to be silent. Then one of the boys started wailing. It was a scream I haven't heard the likes of since. It was like—like—"

"Like what?"

Sammy, deeply confused, looked at Ms. Stetson. "What was I talking about? My mind has gone blank."

"What do you mean?"

"I can't remember what I was talking about!"

"Oh, please, must you resort to games?"

"I'm not playing games. I can't remember what the fuck I was talking about. Now, stop accusing me, or I'll crack open your goddamn skull!" He raised the oak paddle over his head in a furious motion, flipping water into the air. "I'm sick and tired of people not believing me."

"You were talking about the schoolhouse," she shot back. "You mentioned a scream."

"Oh, God, I don't want to talk about it. I can't."

"What did it sound like?" she shouted.

"Ms. Stetson—"

"You need to finish your story, Sammy. We all have a right to know."

"It was like his soul was being dragged out of his body!" He leaned toward her.

"And you know what we did? We had to choose between getting shot or sending that boy out into the cold. So we picked him up over our heads. He didn't struggle. He just needed to cry, that was all. He was just cold and missed home—not being able to stop the flood of grief from his heart was his only crime. But we picked him up and threw him out into the wind to—"

"To what? What happened to him?"

"It was as cold as Alaska. What do you think happened to him?"

SAMMY SNIFFED THE AIR. "WHAT is that horrible smell?"

The canoeists came upon a large flat rock, which forced all the water to move through one five-foot-wide slit almost at the westerly bank. The canoe quickly fell through the slit, and the travelers ferried themselves into a large pool, where the water, because of the boulder, was relatively still. There, dozens upon dozens of dead fish floated.

"Let's paddle around," Sammy said.

In the shallower regions, they could see piles of half-rotted fish. She unpacked her Leica and snapped photos of the kill.

"It smells like a furniture store filled with dead fish. What do you think it is, Sammy?" Ms. Stetson questioned.

"That railway-tie yard a little ways off from shore. It's the third time this summer I've seen it like this, but never this bad."

"They must be dumping their treatment—"

"Look!" Sammy pointed downstream, at the giant northern red-bellied water snake, now listlessly floating on its side beside a rock.

"They must have just dumped a huge load into the water," Rachel realized.

"Between that and having a hook just pulled out of his jaw—"

They paddled to where the red snake floated, its midsection caught by the rock, its head and tail trying to drift downstream.

Sammy placed his hand again around the dying snake's neck and pulled all six feet of it into their canoe.

"I don't understand. I didn't think water snakes grew that large around here," Rachel wondered.

"Just like anything. Every now and then there's a big of everything." Sammy then hugged that fat long reptile, placed the side of its head against his cheek, and snapped its neck.

Ms. Stetson, in her soggy calico dress, saw the boy she used to babysit, decades ago, before the fight against fascism swept her away from Concord. "Sammy—"

"That's all I can say about Korea, Rachel." They left the pool and ventured forth downstream.

"WELL, I'LL BE—" RACHEL SMILED. They looked ahead and saw, in the middle of a small island in the river, a hundred black vultures feasting on a dead, dark brown bull.

"George's vultures." Sammy smiled, too.

The golden afternoon sky was filled with black fliers. The birds' silhouettes cut into space.

"There is just not enough room in his mind for Korea." Sammy nodded.

"HAS BEING BACK IN CONCORD helped you?" Ms. Stetson asked as they both got out of his truck at his store.

He looked at her, the red sun behind him. "It has been over a decade since I was tossed back from Korea, and you are the first person in this town to ask me about what happened over there."

"I doubt that is true."

"To hell it isn't. And you know what? You are the first person, anywhere, to ask about my wounds. Coming back, the army just wanted to know if we had collaborated or not. Yeah, a green CID army major was intent on getting proof out of me that I was a collaborating, brainwashed American. One morning, on the ship ride across the Pacific, he asked me if I'd ever fucked my mother. Not 'How are you? How are your joints? Do you need a dentist? Sorry about being starved for three goddamn years.' But 'Have you ever fucked your mother?' "

"What did you say?"

"No. But I'd love to fuck yours."

"Sammy—"

"Don't get all high and mighty with me. You may be ready to wave the war flag right now. But you, and nobody else, for that matter, was tossing pom-poms welcoming George and me back." He brought his tongue through the hole in his smile created by his missing canine. "I can't even get the VA to give me disability."

"What about the boys who decided not to come home?"

"Jesus, if you were a colored boy from Alabama or Virginia and the Chinese offered you an education as far as you could go, what would you do?

"That damn Eisenhower thought that it was a disgrace that no one escaped the camps. Escape where? It was like the moon.

"There was no place to go—but to hope. And those of us who could, did." Sammy rolled a joint and lit it. He puffed, as if he were sucking in life. Breathing out, he let the smoke settle around him. The sun had set. The remains of daylight refracted over the old womanly mountains.

"So what do you say to the sons of Virginia being sent to Vietnam?"

Sammy looked into the milkweed-strewn field behind his store, where the fireflies lit the air yellow green. "You're not going to just go over there and blow your guns.

"It's war. And you know what?" he whispered. "The worst part is coming home and feeling abandoned. As if all that murder meant nothing."

THAT EVENING, MS. STETSON SAT in her jigsaw house's living room. She read from a noted book about the conflict.

> In every war but one that the United States has fought, the conduct of those of its servicemen who were captured and held in enemy prison camps presented no unforeseen problems . . . and gave rise to no particular concern in the country as a whole. [In only one] was there a wholesale breakdown and wholesale collaboration of the captives with the captors. Moreover . . . in every war but one a respectable number of prisoners managed . . . to escape. That one war was the Korean War. . . .

Trembling in her long cobalt nightgown, she held the book along with her notes and tapes from her canoe ride with Sammy

Nolon. She walked onto her front porch. Looking up at the satellite-staked heavens, the Victorian houses around her, the quiet small-town street, she listened for truth. The night wind came, and she let it scatter her papers into the dark. Her records from the day reeled around her.

AND THEN SHE SCREAMED.

ACROSS TOWN, MRS. GRAVES, MS. Tzigane, and Mr. Silversmith—each in a private nightmare—woke up screaming as well. Sammy heard them.

"It sounded like the soul-cry I witnessed in the schoolhouse during the Tiger Death March."

III

The Stone Carver

"GO ON, GET," PROFESSOR RAYBURN commanded the spear-sized black snake trying to squirm into his front door. While his cats fought off its entry into his stucco house, Rayburn ran into his living room, lifted his bayoneted-rifle off the mantel, and then, after ordering his cats to scatter, stabbed the snake through the head. Its black tongue slid out of its mouth as it fell into death. "Lord, what is going on here?" The history professor wiped his forehead.

"BACK, DAHLIA," TOM DORIAN TOLD his girl. Though the creek was still too frigid to jump in, they had come to this swimming hole to dip their feet. But as they were caressing each other on a gray rock jutting out from the shore, thirteen black snakes emerged from the sycamore roots behind them. One snake wormed through their embraced bodies. Quickly grabbing it by the tail,

Tom smashed its head on the rock. He then proceeded to use the serpent, like a whip, to beat off the encroaching battalion. Now the snake-whip in his hand was falling apart, and its slashes were no longer painful to its brethren—despite the presence of blood. So, black-as-ink Tom Dorian threw down the whip, picked up his redheaded Dahlia, and then forded across the running chill of Lime Creek.

"BEHOLD!" WANDA NOLON PREACHED TO a group of Pentecostals enthusiastically meeting at her cedar house. "I give unto you power to tread on serpents. . . ." She had invited several of the black snakes inside her living room. The serpents nuzzled through her dirty-blond hair, which fell to her ankles.

"And these signs shall follow those who believe," Wanda bellowed. "In my name they shall cast out devils; they shall speak with new tongues; They shall take up serpents; and . . . it shall not hurt them. . . ."

"LADIES AND GENTLEMEN, THIS IS Rachel Stetson reporting from Concord, Virginia—a small town in the Shenandoah Valley—where Jethro O'Pitcans, the town fool, has unearthed one of the most spectacular archeological finds of modern times. He found it in a mine shaft, a mine shaft that he had dug years ago with the hopes of finding coal. A mine shaft that he created because, he claims, the Virgin Mary had told him to. After digging a hundred or so feet, his machines hit a cavern, and he'd given up. But recently, he has returned to the pit and found what the Virgin Mary intended him to search for."

* * *

WEEKS BEFORE RACHEL'S REPORTING BEGAN, it had been a late night and Jethro O'Pitcans couldn't sleep. He'd been up, trying to carve one of the stones he'd picked out of his quarry. He wanted to create a work of great faith and meaning. He even had foolish ambitions of picking out something like the *Pietà* he'd seen engravings of. Perhaps, he hoped, he'd sculpt a man with unshakable purpose. But, try as he might to carve, no figure within the stone spoke. The Lord did not give him a vision.

He fell onto his three-quarters bed. Though he had been tired, now he felt wide awake on that cool March night. He tossed and turned on his horsehair mattress, which he'd inherited from his great-aunt Mrs. O'Lancy—a woman who called purchasing antiques her form of sex. Jethro wondered whether or not he'd have an easier time sleeping if someone were next to him. Since he'd never had a long-term gal, he wasn't sure. Some of the women he'd been with squirmed too much. Others heated up like little furnaces as they slept. All had complained of his unwillingness to hold them in slumber. And, though his birthday was in early December—making him a Sagittarian—he exhibited the signs of being a cold, distant Aquarius. His ghost-gray eyes pierced hearts like moonbeams. Then, when he looked away, the world felt completely black.

Above Jethro's headboard, a hazy rain misted through the window. He rolled more, cursing his mind for falling out of dream and not wanting to stay with his exhausted body in sleep. Then, suddenly, he felt summoned. It was the woman of his childhood cave, who'd told him to dig in the mine shaft. He sat up. His thin, soft sheet fell from his hairless chest. A breeze blew into the room, but he didn't catch a chill. He jumped out of the high bed, slipped his three-ribbed thermoplastic hard hat off the bedpost, fastened it under his chin, and put on his overalls and boots. From his garage, he grabbed his shovel, pick, and carbide lamp. He then marched to the on-site house of his head workman, Toad Wells, and dragged his bony body out of bed.

Having removed the cage years ago from the now-defunct mine shaft, Jethro had Toad position the crane near the hole as he removed the metal covering. Then, Toad hooked Jethro up to a harness attached to the crane's cable.

An energy overcame Jethro as Toad slowly lowered him into the pit. When he reached the church-sized cavernous bottom, where moist cool air flowed, Jethro clenched his pick and started to dig. He didn't know when, or if, he was going to stop, but the flying rocks delighted him. Some of the pieces hit his square face, protected by eyewear and his blond beard. Seeing the ground open up brought fire to his soul. He chipped through a thin layer of calcite. He was about to order Toad to send down a jackhammer when the carbide lamp hissed.

Jethro laughed like a child upon finding buried treasure. His laughter floated through the air like a feather, ready to tickle even deaf ears. He knelt down and swept away the dirt with his hand, exposing a piece of something embedded in the limestone. Spitting on it, he used his finger to polish the unknown. As he chipped away the purple stone from one end, more emerged. Even though he was exhausted, the more he dug, the more he wanted to open the Earth.

Outside the pit, Venus—the morning star—greeted azurite Dawn over the Blue Ridge Mountains. He hammered through the day. Toad followed all orders, hauling stones away from the hole's mouth, bringing Jethro jerky and water. Otherwise, he snoozed unconcerned in the crane cab. By dusk—when Venus appeared again—Jethro had removed enough stone to know that what he'd rediscovered was mammoth. Exhausted, sore, but exhilarated, he looked down at his find, the lamp flickering its flame tongue in his hand as he raised it. He smiled.

He was thinking of carving into the stone the opening of his favorite biblical book, the Gospel of John, the one that inspired him to achieve:

In the beginning was the Word. . . .

"Wouldn't Mom be proud." He beamed, bittersweet, as he worked.

"NOW, THE STORY OF JETHRO O'Pitcans does not begin with this excavation," Rachel explained into her Ampex Model 200 tape recorder. "His story actually begins decades ago, when a ten-year-old Jethro reached headlines throughout the Commonwealth through an article written by my father, Cy Stetson. A young Jethro had ventured into a cave near his house and fallen through the roof of a cavern, hitting his head. In the complete blackness, he shouted for nearly an hour. Cold and sightless, he grappled around the underground.

"In the article, the young Jethro spoke about how he missed his mother, a woman who first thought she was going through the change when she conceived Jethro. A woman whose even older husband, Jethro's father, had died to leave her to raise Jethro alone. Yet in the darkness, Jethro remembered the biblical lessons she'd helped him learn. He couldn't understand why God would have gone through all the trouble to have her bear him if he was just going to die alone in a cave.

"He suddenly saw a woman with dark long hair and a tan gown. Smiling, she told him to follow her. The ten-year-old Jethro grabbed her dress and squirmed behind her, with the cold spring water, for over a hundred yards of tunnels. For a long time, rough stones brushed his shoulders and blond hair.

"He came to a space where he could reach up high and feel nothing. He described being taken through a two-foot pool, where he touched squishy planarians, scurrying crayfish, and crunchy centipedes. Thirsty, he felt he'd sinned because he'd wandered too far from home. She had him drink the calcium-rich waters and rebaptize himself; then she led him much farther.

"He could no longer see his guide. But ahead he saw a light. It was gray-eyed dusk right outside of Angel Falls.

"Since then, Jethro O'Pitcans has always been the town fool. For instance, that evening, stitching up his head in the hospital, Dr. Brothers told him he was damn lucky, and in the future he'd better not leave home without a helmet. The next day, his mother took him to the hardware store and bought him a hard-boiled hat. He's been wearing that hat, or one of its replacements, ever since.

"And on more than one occasion, he has sought to inspire the townfolks with the Word. Every Good Friday, he dresses himself in a robe, puts on a crown of wineberry stems, and wanders the streets of Concord with a cross on his back. But, perhaps even more noticeable, he's taken up carving many of the formations around Concord. For instance, out by the Fork Cliffs—where youngsters often park—he's carved the rockface to look like the Virgin Mary."

CARVING OUT HIS MOST RECENT find, Jethro recited the psalms that his mother had taught him after that first miraculous escape from the cave decades ago.

> I waited patiently for the Lord; and He inclined to me, and heard my cry.
>
> He also brought me up out of a horrible pit, out of the miry clay, and set my feet upon a rock and established my steps.
>
> He has also put a new song in my mouth—praise to our God. . . .

When Jethro's mother died his sophomore year of high school, it was not clear what would happen to him. Yet Rachel Stetson had sat next to him in geometry class, seen he was very good at numbers, and enlisted him to help with her homework. When she saw in the school art show his raw, choppy sculpture with three heads (one bearded, one smooth faced, and another with a sheet over his eyes), she was amused by his depiction of the trinity. Everyone else thought it was just the deranged musings of a boy who'd hit his head too hard as a child.

Rachel convinced her father, owner of the *Concord Gazette,* to take the kid in. Yet in the house he moved around silently, left cabinets and drawers open, played with the calico cat, or was outside in the shed, chipping away at stones. He'd broken apart hundreds before he found the beginnings of his first warped saint.

And while he worked, he would keen, shifting from side to side or back and forth—even though Cy Stetson lectured that it made him appear witless. And Rachel would often hear Jethro praying,

"Many, O Lord, are Your wonderful works. . . . If I would declare and speak, they are more than can be numbered. . . ."

"NOW, JETHRO O'PITCANS, THOUGH MANY consider him an odd fellow, is not your normal town fool," Rachel continued to record.

"He has been described as one of the most brilliant students ever to graduate from the civil engineering department at the Southern Military Institute. During the War, while his classmates and friends, like Toad Wells, were sent off to battle, the professors at the Institute arranged a job for him mining Colorado Plateau sandstone. And in those large open holes, larger than the ancient Roman amphitheaters, it occurred to him that quarrying was the best thing to do with the exhausted, in-debt, thin-soiled two-hundred-acre farm his mother had left him—land everyone commented was worthless because it was full of stones.

"One quarry he's now created has a mouth the size of a football field and is six or seven stories deep. Every now and then, he'll find a piece of rock that he wants to carve, perhaps it is decked here and there with pyrite. And he'll take the stone and do his best to carve a saint that he'd prayed to with his mother, whom he hopes had loved him.

"Indeed, through his art, Jethro desired to show what his mother had taught him, that, to quote the Gospel, 'All things were made through Him, and without Him nothing was made that was made.'

"Yet Jethro's sales of his own sculpture have not gone well. The most anyone ever paid was when Alistair MacGregor bought Jethro's life-sized scupture of Saint Francis of Assisi and declared, 'He'll make one hell of a scarecrow.'

"Besides that sculpture, Mr. O'Pitcans has also picked out an image of Saint Anthony with a kaleidoscope of lost things emerging from his body. And Saint Elmo, with electrical discharges shooting from his hair.

"'If they weren't already with Jesus, I think your art would bring the saints up from their graves,' Mrs. MacJenkins once remarked to Jethro. Hurt, Jethro spent a week hiding in the woods."

* * *

BACK IN THE PIT, JETHRO reflected about how he had always wanted to be a sculptor, like Michelangelo, or the Greeks with their Laocoön masterpiece. For with the works of art, he wanted to show beauty; and it was through beauty he felt he could give a sense of the Lord.

> I delight to do Your will, O my God . . .
> Indeed, I do not restrain my lips . . .

Jethro continued to brush at the remains. He felt them more impressive than the *Pietà*. They brought to mind stories his mother had told him of a German nun, whose grave, feared robbed, was opened six weeks after her death—yet her body was fresh. The nun, like Jethro, had been born poor and had religious visions. Jethro pictured the stigmata that were said to have opened on the nun's wrists, feet, and forehead. He wondered if they'd also appear on his mounted relic. He wished his find would come alive and—bleeding or not—like a holy spirit sweep him away to a time and place he didn't know but wanted to know because he felt like such a fool. Why is it that someone is considered witless if he has lofty ambitions to show his faith in God?

"And the light shines in the darkness," he thought, "and the darkness did not comprehend it."

Continuing to sand the remains, he did not know what to think. For in the matrix, he'd see a piece of what looked like moss, or fern, and he remembered when "God said, Let the earth bring forth grass, the herb yielding seed, and the fruit tree . . ." But he saw no grasses, no seeds. . . .

Jethro marched into the nearby woods, where he cut down

the last remaining giant cherry tree left in his forest. He split the trunk lengthwise right down the middle. After calling Rachel Stetson on the phone again, he lowered the pieces into the pit.

A few hours later, she stood in a gray drizzle, contemptuously looking at Toad Wells, the youngest of fifteen children. She marveled at how he could be content just sitting in a crane cab for his life.

"Rachel, I want to show you what I have found," Jethro pleaded when he emerged, his wet blond bangs over his eyes.

"Is that why you called me? To take me down into some hole?"

"You are the only person—"

"Jethro, I don't have time for this. Everyone wants me to report on these strange snake incidents. Alistair MacGregor says he's resorted to using a blowtorch to fight off the serpents from his chicken coops. He's even started praying to Saint Patrick. You might try selling sculptures of *him* right now." She walked away.

"This has something to do with the snakes."

She looked back. "Are you fooling me?"

"No photographs. You can't tell anyone. Something is off about this. And I don't want people laughing at me like they do with the sculptures. Just you, me, and this marvel."

TOAD HOOKED THEIR THIRTY-TWO-YEAR-OLD BODIES up to the crane. They sunk to the pit's bottom—to the cavern. There, Jethro grabbed Rachel by the hand and led her a few paces. He knelt and turned off his carbide lamp. After removing his gloves, he kissed his Southern Military Institute class ring, which he'd set with his mother's diamond. With his hard hat still on, he closed his eyes and began to pray.

"I have not hidden Your righteousness within my heart. . . ."

Jethro thought about what had been the purpose of his life, why he aspired to be a great sculptor, and he awed at the thing before him.

"For the law was given through Moses, but grace and truth came through Jesus Christ," he remembered his mother telling him.

PLEASED TO FIND JETHRO DISTRACTED, Rachel moved away from him. Focusing her headlamp on the thing before her, she quickly pulled out her notebook and scribbled—

Pinned on a cherry wood cross
Wings, spread wide, the size of a B52 bomber
Claws halfway down them, extended giant pinky
Skin-like impressions everywhere
Head like a massive horse-pelican
Huge dark eye sockets
Sail like antler
Human ribs
Twisted and turned about itself

". . . O LORD." JETHRO ASKED, "LET YOUR Loving-kindness and Your truth continually preserve me." And he remembered, with fear, when "God said, Let the waters bring forth abundantly the fowl that may fly above the earth . . ." But was this a bird? Jethro wondered. This did not look at all like—

THEN RACHEL SAW THE SNAKES, hundreds of them, whirling around the awesome fossil as it gave them warmth and power.

They were coming and going from the cavern, no doubt from several entrances around Concord.

"WILL YOU BE HERE TOMORROW?" she asked as they rose to the surface. Her dark hair frazzled about her head, despite all the bobby pins she'd used.

"Yes." Jethro trembled. Almost subconsciously, he placed her palm on his face. "I will be praying down there all day and thinking about it. Please tell no one. I'll come up around dusk."

AT DUSK THE NEXT DAY, Rachel Stetson and a hundred or so townies waited for Jethro to emerge from his pit. Rachel had worked through the night to make the tapes you heard earlier about Jethro's past, as well as to run a story about his find in her paper. She had also sent the material to her old bosses during the War at CBS radio, including Edward R. Murrow, in hopes that he would be taken with her story of a small-town fool. But she needed more tapes. . . .

"This is Rachel Stetson. I am back at the mine shaft of Jethro O'Pitcans," Rachel recorded. "A hundred or so townies have gathered to see the source of the serpents slithering around their town. People like Sammy Nolon. Sammy, can you tell us about your recent encounter with the black snake?"

"Well, George and I were about to shoot a bunny rabbit the other day, but a black snake ate it."

"Thank you, Sammy. The sun is now setting, and Toad Wells is beginning to raise the crane. We can see the top of Jethro's head—"

The chatter in the crowd suddenly fell silent. Rachel grasped the sandalwood beaded necklace she wore.

"Jethro is covered. Large serpents are wrapped around his head like black turbans. Others coil around his neck. Hissing pythons wrangle over his shoulders and cling to his chest. Small ones even intermingle in his hands and bootlaces. Yet still, he seems calm.

"Toad, eerily numb about it all, lifts Jethro high above the pit, moving him a few yards from the mouth, and then lowers him to the earth. The serpents move from his face.

"Now Jethro opens his arms. He opens his arms like Christ himself—wide and strong. He stumbles a few paces and looks at the crowd."

Jethro yelled as if he could have cracked Deadman Mountain with his voice. The snakes fell from his body. He collapsed.

THE NEXT AFTERNOON, JETHRO O'PITCANS woke to someone poking him on his left shoulder. He opened his eyes. Rachel Stetson sat on the edge of his bed. She uncharacteristically—and with some spite—applied her lipstick. Hazel Bishop, Dark Red, Kissable. "Hello, Jethro."

Jethro didn't say anything.

"Jethro, they needed to know. You have to learn to open your life. That's your problem." She forced her small mouth to smile.

He kept his gray eyes downcast.

"There are some people outside, by the mine shaft, who'd like to see you." She pursed her lips.

He noticed his shutters were closed from outside.

"They are not leaving until you come out. So unless you want them to stay here forever."

Resisting the urge to shake his head, Jethro closed his eyes.

"Come on, Sleeping Beauty, you've had more than enough rest." She left his room and went outside.

JETHRO GOT OUT OF BED. He put on his hard hat, clothes, and boots. He left his room and forced himself to swing open his front door.

COUNTLESS THOUSANDS. PEOPLE. EVERYWHERE. LIKE locusts. Droning. There were fearful townspeople. United Daughters of the Confederacy—decked in white, red, and blue—proclaimed the second coming of Robert E. Lee, for even his crypt in Lee Chapel was infested with the fertile monsters. "The South will blossom again!" Gideons passed out Bibles, which some people ripped up to make nests for the serpents. The Mormons from Bassville preached that the black snakes were cursed black because they were "the posterity of Cain." Jehovah's Witnesses, angry no one was home to hear their knocking, blamed the darkness on the curse Noah placed upon those of Canaan. Members of the KKK, robed in white, cried the serpents represented the appendages of the colored men, like Tom Dorian, who desired to defile our white women. Twelve black vultures perched on Rachel's charcoal Studebaker. A hundred or so Pentecostals assembled in choir fashion and spoke in tongues almost as unintelligible as Yankee.

Jethro froze. Rachel took a deep breath. Her eyes, like those of a horned owl, widened. She knew her old bosses at CBS had someone watching. With the help of Sheriff Wineland, Rachel had made sure she was the only official reporter close to Jethro. But it would not last long. She had to complete this story fast.

"He's risen alive!" Rachel Stetson cheered into the microphone, set up on Jethro's front porch. The audience burst again in a droning mix of strife and celebration. Rachel stepped back and took a photo of Jethro's back silhouetted by the exuberant mass. She then stepped forward again. "And Jethro," Rachel asked, "what have you done to make snakes rise from the pit? Is the Virgin Mary appearing to you again, after all these years?"

He timidly stepped toward the microphone and softly spoke. "Let me go back down again and find out."

"Hallelujah!" Wanda Nolon, draped in black snakes, shot up and began to dance in celebration. A few Pentecostals, missing arms or ears, joined her.

AS JETHRO DESCENDED INTO THE pit, his eyes scanned back and forth as he thought about how seeing the layers of stones, folded on top of each other, reminded him of one of the Virginia Woolf novels he'd seen Rachel enjoy, but he couldn't make sense of it, for the past was sometimes folded on top of, sometimes mixed with, the present. Descending into this was like falling into a deep sleep, a world where the unconscious took control of his conscious. A mine shaft that he'd dug in order to find his dreams.

"For innumerable evils have surrounded me; my iniquities have overtaken me, so that I am not able to look up; they are more than the hairs on my head; therefore, my heart fails me. . . ."

Upon reaching the pit's bottom, he again knelt and folded his big bony hands in prayer. In the silent, cool blackness, with no light at the end of no tunnel, he felt peace.

Jethro remembered just coming home from working in the Colorado mines. He read in the paper that Little Boy had just been dropped, unleashing a "rain of ruin from the air the likes of which has never been seen on this Earth." And as he had looked at the article, it became clear to him that the mushroom cloud had been made from the uranium in the sandstone he'd spent the War mining. He had almost thrown up.

As the snakes slithered up his body, Jethro felt a world without guilt, without blame, without a need for forgiveness—for sin does not exist. Violence. Freedom.

The Virgin Mary appeared, with serpents in her hair. She embraced him. He felt her mane slithering against his lips, earlobes, and jaw. And he knew that at the Place of the Skull, she had wanted to answer her son's question. She also wished that she could have jumped, flown up to the cross, and ripped out the nails in his arms and feet. Then, with her son on her back, she could have soared away from Jerusalem, God, time, and written culture—to where no salmon-pink stone building society existed. Jesus did not have to be a revolutionary, just as Jethro did not have to be considered a fool. He could just have been her son, she his ma, and they could have lived by the sea and in the giant fern, cycad, or coniferous trees. A landscape without grass, seeds, or fruits—just green. Then, as she hugged Jethro, Mary hissed into his ears a story.

He saw the being he had resurrected soaring, with wings almost the size of an *Enola Gay* bomber, when a great asteroid smashed into this planet and sent a nuclear-scale dust cloud into the atmosphere. That great flying reptile, once part of an aerial armada, knew that a holocaust was happening. But it kept on flying, through the ashy air, because it loved to fly.

When the pterosaur landed in an estuary, as its world was coming to an end, it lay down in a streambed. The floodwaters rolled it over, onto its back. It was tired, so it just let itself be buried in small fragments. The water yielded minerals to its bones—saving the shape of its cells. The sea life to come would then cast it in a deep bed of blue limestone. Upon which Rock, Concord would be built.

It had been the end of an era longer than civilization could hope for. Of creatures the size of temples. Without the ability to report about the past, the present, or the future.

"In the beginning God created Heaven and Earth. In the beginning was the Word and the Word was with God, and the Word was God."

But this creature, Jethro knew, was before all Words.

Jethro was losing consciousness. Two small snakes had bitten him with their hypodermic fangs in his wrists, and he was losing blood. As he felt embraced by the Virgin Mary, he wondered why God would create a world that existed for so long without meaning, where the grandest creatures led to nothing. A world without love, art, pity. Just bones. Bones baptized by Medusa.

The Virgin Mary spoke. "Jethro!" Light burned from her third eye. The snakes were no longer in her hair. She was pulling them from him in a panic, giving her a fear of serpents that she would never recover from.

"Rachel?" he gasped. "I want to stay down here."

"What—?"

"Instead of letting me create a masterwork, God has bestowed upon me this fossil, this spectacular specimen that I have resurrected, which has taken away what used to inspire: the sacred.

"Come back. Mary, come back and don't abandon me. Fight off this flying reptile. This thing that spreads his arms in crucifixion wider than Jesus! It was more real and ancient than all the prophets combined. And it flew—like an angel."

"Jethro," Rachel forced herself to ask, looking at him, "what did—?"

Like a ghost also forgotten by religion, he looked at her and uttered, "The Fool has said in heart, 'There is no God.' They are corrupt, they have done abominable works, there is none who does good."

Sobbing and covered in grime, he crawled away from the crucified pterosaur as he finished the psalm sarcastically:

> Let them be confounded because of their shame, who say to me,
> "Aha, aha!"
> . . . The Lord be magnified!
> . . . do not delay. O my God.

Then, he finished with a prayer that came from he knew not where.

> Who will have me? Who will be with me?
> Here I stand: will you take me? I am a singer . . .
> Great are the stones as I carve them . . . they are my song.

"Without a psalm to sing, I no longer live."

He slunk into a nearby two-foot-deep pool and started cleansing himself. Taking his helmet off, he submerged his whole being before coming back up. He didn't protest when the flash from Rachel's Leica camera illuminated the giant fossil and his stark face.

In the cold water around him, he felt the squishy planarians, scurrying crayfish, and crunchy centipedes. Bowing his head forward, he lapped the calcium-rich waters. Despite the loss of a name to worship or a prayer to invoke—a mystery now haunted Jethro O'Pitcans.

"Rachel, how did I make it out of this cave as a child?" He let himself rock violently.

AND WHEN RACHEL DRAGGED HIM to the surface, all the black snakes—except the one Professor Rayburn just stabbed with his bayoneted rifle—had slithered away.

IV

The Heiress

WHEN BETTY JOE LEE DEBUTT Carlisle shot her father, William, she blew a hole right through his back and out his sternum. By ten o'clock the next day, Sheriff Wineland filed a report stating that the incident was clearly an accident. The case was closed for good. The following Wednesday, when Ms. Stetson's *Concord Gazette* came out, she didn't mention a word.

The Carlisles stunk of money. The smell had permeated their being ever since William's granddaddy, Eli, made a fortune in railroad speculation up North. Shortly afterwards, he came carpetbagging down to Virginia and bought up most of our town. Their main house is up yonder, on Big Hill, just east of Concord. It's the big limestone plantation house on seventy-five acres. You can see it's surrounded by those rusty juniper trees.

When he was young, Betty Joe's father was the best-looking boy in town. Besides a small scar, which Blanche LeBlanc had bestowed onto his left cheek, he had beautiful skin. Tall and lanky, he looked like a real English gentleman, except he had excellent teeth. He was not, however, the brightest fellow. By donating some land to Jefferson College, which is right here in Concord, William's father bribed the school into taking him. There, William distinguished himself as an ambitious drinker. He was also a member of the college's sacred secret society, the Corpses. We know this because one morning Ms. Violet Graves, the Carlisles' property manager, found him passed out naked in their foyer, and she saw the signature skull-brand on his buttock. He never let anyone else look at his fanny.

When William graduated from Jefferson, he settled down to take care of the family business. As he saw it, there wasn't much to do other than order Violet to accumulate rents. He spent his days collecting money; playing golf; or hunting bear, deer, beaver, duck, raccoon, turkey, possum, rabbit, squirrel, and whatever else he could shoot at. He was a late riser, early setter, and took pleasure in at least one nap per day.

Betty Joe's mother was none other than Catherine Lee deButt, a direct descendant of Robert E. Lee. See, Robert E. Lee Jr. didn't have any boys. But one of his daughters, Mary Curtis, married a deButt and attached "Lee" to the front of her children's last names. As far as we know, there are no more Lees that are direct descendants of the General. There are, though, the Lee deButts.

When Catherine Lee deButt was twelve, her father dropped dead from a heart attack. The expenses of raising a family without a daddy drained what was left of her share of the Lee deButt coffers dry. To help pay the bills, they sold their home's front yard to the United States Government. That's why the big post office is there now.

Catherine Lee deButt possessed skin almost as white as the bleached Blanche LeBlanc and her daughter Mary Anne, whom most considered to be albinos. Catherine, though, had jet-black hair, milky-white skin, and bore a striking resemblance to Walt Disney's Snow White. She looked particularly like Snow White when she wore one of her ocher dresses, which she sewed herself. When Catherine reached marrying age, she realized she and her momma were in trouble. She also knew of only one man in town with the money to help her out. So a year after she graduated from Hollins College, she hitched herself to Concord's aging playboy, William Carlisle.

Little did she know it would have been easier to extract money from William's grandfather Eli, who was cold and moldering in the Stonewall Jackson Cemetery. William moved in with Catherine and her mother into the Lee deButt House behind the post office. But he wouldn't pay to fix even a leaking sink or toilet. Within a few years, the kitchen floor had rotted out because he'd refused to pay a plumber to fix a pipe. When the handle on the downstairs commode broke, William thought it was perfectly customary to make people lift off its back and use a wrench to release the water after relieving themselves. Our Snow White had married a bona fide, good-for-nothing leech, who loved to hoard his money for no reason other than he was a self-centered, self-indulgent son of a—

Catherine had to get herself a job as a secretary with the young district attorney, Mr. Cummings, so she could help her momma try to keep up the family's antebellum brick house. Catherine's ma had a stroke and keeled over. We're sure it was because of the stress William put her through. Still, Snow White had to work even while she was big and pregnant.

Once William's father—Old Man Henry Carlisle—died, William, Catherine, and their ten-year-old daughter, Betty Joe, moved from the Lee deButt House to the more capacious limestone mansion on Big Hill. William was now the owner of over half the real estate in town, all bringing in good rents. Though he possessed enough spare bills to wipe his fanny with, he wouldn't take care of his buildings—even as their rents started declining. He let that beautiful Lee deButt House go to ruin. One winter, the heater broke, and he declined to pay for its repair. The family renting the house moved out. The pipes then froze and burst.

There was only so much that Catherine Lee deButt could handle. The day after the pipes in her former home burst, she went down to see Helen Hart, the meanest, finest divorce lawyer in the Commonwealth. Helen told her that the court judgment would be in her favor. Everyone knew William Carlisle cringed every time he had to reach inside his back pocket, and Concord was in decay because of him. Helen's brother, Otis, had recently moved out of a place he'd rented from the Carlisles for fifteen years. The septic tank had clogged, and William wouldn't pay to have it emptied, so Otis's yard was always filled with poop.

It was not only his cheapness that put people off. William had taken an even stronger affection for the bottle than he had at Jefferson. On the golf course, he was often seen taking long swigs straight from a fresh bottle of Colonel's Pride bourbon.

One day while practicing his drive at the edge of his yard, under the elderly juniper trees, he hit a ball so wildly that it careened toward Mrs. Elise MacJenkins's living room window while she was hosting a bridge game. "The cards foretell of a hostile visitor," Ms. Tzigane had warned. The white orb then crashed into the room and plopped into Mary Anne Randolph's teacup. William denied responsibility, even though sixteen respectable women saw him beating apart Elise's azalea bushes in search of his lost ball.

Catherine Lee deButt was going to win this divorce case. The judge, Mr. Tuttwild, had lived for many years next door to the Lee deButt home. He was not pleased with the manner in which

William had treated Catherine or her house. We all looked forward to the divorce because we knew that she would take care of her half of the Carlisle property.

It was an icy Wednesday night in early March when Catherine went home from Helen Hart's. Who knows what happened that night in the limestone plantation mansion? The next morning, Dr. Harris and his team of nurses hauled our Snow White out on a stretcher—covered by a white sheet. William claimed she'd become drunk and violent, and he, in self-defense, shot her with his engraved E. Lefaucheux French pinfire revolver. Whatever occurred, Catherine put up a great fight. According to Sheriff Wineland, the blood trail showed that after Catherine was shot, she yanked Lee's saber off the mantel and, in a final gust of strength, axed off William's right hand.

Since the only possible witness was the ten-year-old Betty Joe, there wasn't much we could do. As Mr. Cummings, the district attorney, confessed, "How do you take to trial a one-handed man with more money than the rest of town?"

Catherine had it set up so that when she died, any money from the sale of the Lee deButt estate went directly to Betty Joe, who, under the guidance of Elise MacJenkins, used the funds carefully for her personal development. Like her mother, she loved to ride. William would have refused to buy her a donkey. One day, though, she was jogging by Lime Creek when a bony, starved horse inside a barbed-wire enclosure trotted up beside her. She stopped, and he halted as well. Over the rusted fence, he stared at her with his large dragonfly-like eyes. Even though his glare was a bit overwhelming, she kept staring back. He did not look away, and she saw in him bravery. His coat would have been a bright white except it had black blotches dribbled here and there, as if it had been defiled by Jackson Pollock.

Betty Joe approached the shack near the field. Potbellied and shirtless, Eugene Wells answered the door and told her he was holding the animal for his cousin Benjy, who planned on hauling it to the meat market in a few days.

"How much is that horse's meat worth?" Betty Joe inquired.

"Well, he might be thin, but he's big. I'd say at least thirty dollars."

"I'll give you the money this afternoon. You can tell Benjy that the meat market swung by and picked up the animal."

"I'll give him twenty-five and tell him I ate it," Eugene said, smiling.

The horse was wild, jumping with each step. The initial weeks she owned him, Betty Joe was out every night looking for the beast, who'd leap out of his stall window and across the driveway's cattle guards.

The first show she took him to, the horse decided he had enough after the first event. When she dismounted, the animal took off toward town. Betty Joe followed as fast as she could. As she ran through Professor Rayburn's backyard, he mistook her tan riding suit for skin and called up the Sheriff to report that a well-shaped, naked maiden had just galloped through his sunflower patch. Sheriff Wineland naturally felt that call was more pressing than the reports flooding in of a wild horse and scampered out in hot pursuit of the runaway nudist. Meanwhile, Simon Donald, who grows the best flowers around, was allowing the Concord Bridge Club to play among his rosebushes when that charger galloped through. The steed stopped and looked with deep interest at the women while they continued their game. Mrs. MacJenkins shushed the animal, as she and Ms. Tzigane were about to win the rubber. When they claimed victory, the horse jumped back and forth over Simon's prize-winning Queen Anne rosebushes as the old women watched and cheered. The stallion then cantered off. Eventually, he was caught, exhausted and sunbathing in the middle of Main Street—not at all concerned that he'd backed up cars for all four blocks of it—from the Stonewall Jackson Cemetery to Mr. Silversmith's Jewelry Exchange and Watch Repair Shop. The Concord Bridge Club sent Betty Joe a card saying they very much enjoyed meeting her horse. They suggested she name him Snail Shadow, since he liked gardens so much.

Betty Joe kept Snail Shadow because she liked the idea of molding something from raw talent, and he was one hell of a jumper. Ms. Tzigane gave Betty Joe lessons. In exchange, Betty Joe helped Ms. Tzigane perform physical therapy on her handicapped animals, like her three-legged dancing black bear, Cassandra, or her paraplegic dachshund, Clea. Betty Joe also stabled other people's horses at her place and used the money to keep up the barn and Snail Shadow. People liked being at her place because she ran such a clean barn. There wasn't a lazy bone in that girl's hard body.

IN ABOUT A YEAR, SHE had transformed Snail Shadow from a wild horse to a fine showman. When the three-day Barbara Blue Show came around at the Virginia Horse Center north of town, she entered. We were hopeful but, honestly, didn't think she'd perform well with that meat-market-bound horse. No one from Concord had ever won the Barbara Blue. The elusive victory seemed a humiliation fixed to the town's personality.

Well, you wouldn't have thought that girl was an underdog when she showed up for the first event. Betty Joe had her long dirty-blond hair pulled back in a tight French braid and had polished every buckle and stirrup so well, light two-stepped off them.

Her navy-blue riding jacket and khaki riding pants were without a crease, and Ms. Tzigane had tailored them so that they displayed Betty Joe's strong, fit frame. On her feet, she wore beautiful custom leather boots, which Mrs. MacJenkins had bought her. And the steed, that once meat-market-bound stallion, looked so serene, we wondered if Simon Donald, the Botanist, hadn't slipped it a few soothing herbs. Calmly obeying Betty Joe's every command, the horse held third place after the dressage competition. Mrs. MacJenkins called up Ms. Stetson.

The next morning, the entire Concord Bridge Club—in high heels, big hats, and floral dresses—was on the top of the glade where the cross-country course starts. Betty Joe approached the starting line and bowed her head dutifully as the women—each clutching a mint julep—waved back. The bell rang, and Betty Joe took off.

No one questioned anymore whether or not that was the same wild horse. Now he galloped, galloped and jumped to the command of Betty Joe, the daughter of Catherine Lee deButt. She was riding that horse with doubtless ambition over the hills of her forefathers, with the same sure-footedness with which General Lee had ridden Traveller. Snail Shadow was tearing through the land. As Betty Joe crossed the finish line, the wrinkled women of the Concord Bridge Club were jumping up and down, not caring that their high heels were digging deeper into the clay-mud. Damn it, Betty Joe broke the course record!

No one else came close to Betty Joe's time. The men who were in first and second place after the dressage competition became nervous because this whippersnapper had done so well, so they both knocked out rails. Since we'd given up giving a hoot about horse shows, Ms. Stetson ran off a special edition of her paper announcing that "Betty Joe Lee Debutt Carlisle, on that wild, once meat-market-bound horse of hers, is leading in the Barbara Blue competition! SHE MIGHT WIN IT ALL!"

Parents did not let their children go to school; mailmen didn't report to duty; even Sammy Nolon, the Snake Man, who hadn't shut his ammunition-produce-alcohol-fireworks-and-live-bait shop on a weekday since he came back from Korea, closed up. Who cared! Betty Joe might win the Barbara Blue competition and show all those highbrows from Kentucky and Northern Virginia what a girl from Appalachia could do.

The horse center stadium was packed so tight, people were breathing on each other. Everyone was there, even Betty Joe's spoiled father. Steve Pampas squirmed around the stands selling "burgers" and "hot dogs," which we gobbled down. Still, the air smelled of our hunger. When Betty Joe entered the arena, we stood up, cheered, and prayed. She looked at us, stared stone cold at the course in front of her, and began.

It was so quiet, you could hear a mouse fart as Betty Joe and Snail Shadow made it over the jumps and small pits. No one was going to exhale until she overcame that last obstacle—the big fence her top competitors' mounts had nicked with their front hooves. We watched earnestly, praying before each hurdle, gasping after each one, and waiting for the last. How could she do so well? No one from Concord had ever done so well in that ring. We dreaded the last jump. She was only ahead by a few seconds.

Snail Shadow suddenly altered his canter to a high trot, as if he wanted to go wild. Then the steed stopped right in front of the huge, high fence lined with Simon Donald's red Queen Anne rosebushes. The clock ticked. Our hearts fell.

Like a Hindu fakir, Snail Shadow lifted his front legs and

levitated over the rosebushes and six-foot rail. Landing lightly on the other side, he trotted peacefully past the finish line, with a half second to spare. Betty Joe had won.

We burst into tears. The bridge club simultaneously tossed up their huge floral-bedecked hats. Ms. Tzigane ripped open her clothes. Sammy Nolon asked the woman he'd been dating for almost a decade to marry him, and she even accepted. All this was happening as we stormed the sawdust pit. Bawling, rolling, and hugging each other, we tried to touch the sacred, dragonfly-eyed, Pollock-drip-painted beast. They gave Betty Joe the big silver cup and adorned the beautiful Snail Shadow—once marked for dog food—with a yellow tulip sash. She pulled her best friend, Lily Carfield, and Ms. Tzigane from the crowd and hugged them. Betty Joe then stood beside her horse and let us all pet Snail Shadow. Laughing and smiling with us, she applauded him.

BETTY JOE CONTINUED TO RIDE, preparing for the upcoming U.S. National Trials. Meanwhile, her father was still drinking and napping in that limestone mansion up on Big Hill. He grimaced whenever anyone mentioned how great, ambitious, and full of potential his daughter was.

Then one night Snail Shadow got into the grain stall and overate. He needed his stomach pumped out right away. When Betty Joe asked her father for help moving the animal, William refused.

Mrs. Graves, who lived nearby, heard them arguing. Betty Joe ran outside and was attempting to get the horse into the trailer when William, drunk and wearing his threadbare red-plaid robe, stumbled out of the house. "What the hell are you doing? You're not taking that horse to no vet. That damn horse has cost this family a fucking fortune. Get the hell out of my way."

He lifted his engraved revolver and shot Snail Shadow between his large black eyes.

TWO WEEKS LATER, AT THREE o'clock in the afternoon, Simon Donald and District Attorney Cummings parked at the bottom of Big Hill. They crept slowly up the driveway. William was drinking in the study as he listened to the Virginia Tech versus UVA game. While his eyes were closed, Betty Joe came into the room, hid his pistol, and made sure his great gun chests were locked. She slipped the keys into her pocket.

Right as he started to raise his voice at her for making too much noise, Simon Donald and District Attorney Cummings burst into the dark brown study. Quick-like, they jerked the haggard man off his alligator-skin chair and pulled him by his feet down the hall—into his bedroom. The two of them stripped off his clothes and dressed him in his dilapidated hunting coveralls. He howled like an angry, decrepit dog as the District Attorney and the Botanist dragged him down the Victorian cherry staircase, out the front door, and into the yard. There they stood, waiting for Betty Joe to promenade through the front door. When she appeared, she wasn't wearing her hunting outfit. She was wearing her mother's favorite ocher dress—and the boots she herself had worn to win the Barbara Blue.

Betty Joe had two guns. In her left hand, she grasped her father's engraved E. Lefaucheux French pinfire revolver, the one he had used to kill her momma and her horse. Slung over her right shoulder, she had none other than the hunting rifle of her great-great-granddaddy, the General. The Botanist and the District Attorney nodded at the Heiress, and then shoved her one-handed father onto the ground as they ran off. William didn't know why they were running until he glared up and saw his daughter. He recognized his wife's favorite ocher dress—and the pistol Betty Joe waved above her head.

He took off, as fast as an aged drunk man can run, down Big Hill toward Concord. As she stood there, staring at him through her strong royal-blue eyes, she must have been thinking how she had only one shot in her grandsire's musket. If she shot it, she might miss, or hit her father just in the leg. Then she'd have to use the revolver. Sheriff Wineland would have a hard time explaining to any state policeman how Betty Joe had accidentally shot her father with two different guns. But as she looked at the revolver, she thought how she hated that engraved weapon; she desired to despise and bury it forever. All this time, her father was running, crying, and stumbling in his worn coveralls toward Concord. He thought that someone in town might help him—if they heard him weeping.

She took careful aim and fired—hitting her father in the top part of his backbone, right below the neck. The minié ball crashed through the upper regions of his heart, causing him to stumble into the bramble of a wineberry bush. The bullet burst out of his sternum just at the place where the rusty juniper trees begin, and at just that moment, Mrs. MacJenkins and the rest of the Concord Bridge Club sat smiling over their fresh iced tea.

V

The Flag Bearer

EVERY THIRD OF JULY, A day before the town of Concord gathers at the Southern Military Institute's parade ground for our hot air balloon rally and fireworks display, you will find many of the community's most respectable members in Mrs. Violet Graves's front yard.

Mrs. MacJenkins makes a big barrel of her famous firewater.

Simon Donald provides a full vase of violet roses, which he places on the porch.

And out in that yard, we eat kale, black-eyed peas, and whatever else old Violet Graves has cooked up.

In jovial fashion, we ask each other how the summer is going. But as the sun begins to set, Violet with her swollen legs rises up the steps of her baby blue porch. Right when the bottom of the orange summer sun hits Deadman Mountain in the distance, she says, "I want to thank you all for being here." She then picks up a brand-new American flag, which was tightly folded on her porch table. She unfolds it, and the wind flutters the cloth before her—like a loose sail. She holds her steady gaze on its waves. We watch and wait. . . .

VIOLET GRAVES IS THE IMPROBABLE manager for the Carlisle family. She has been in their service her whole life—first serving Eli, then Old Man Henry, William, and now Betty Joe. She thinks, as far as being colored goes, she's had a pleasant bunch of bosses.

See, the Carlisles—with the exception of Betty Joe Lee deButt Carlisle—are not real Southerners. Nor have they ever pretended to be part of the great Slavocracy. Au contraire, Eli met his wife, Mildred Ovington, while they were both attending a lethally liberal Northern college, Oberlin, which was not only co-ed but also let Negroes in. Those liberals didn't see the mischief they'd serve up in teaching a subordinate to think. Mildred, that woman, was a sociologist, and spent much time intellectually arguing with scholars that black people were not indeed, "man children." Alas, when William Sumner published *Folksways* in 1907, she was horrified at how scholars embraced his idea that blacks are preordained ape-brained, folktale-telling, soul-singing fools. Mildred then decided it would be right interesting if a pitch-black girl could expound Virgil, explain Euclid, or recite passages about Melville's White Whale as she walked amongst the humpkins and bumpkins of Concord, Virginia.

Thus, when Geneva, her maid of a few decades, died giving birth to a baby girl, Mildred decided to educate the child. She taught Violet—from birth—mostly sums and science, things that no one thought would fit into a "monkey brain." But that girl sucked it up, like a tropical sponge.

This was all a particularly delicate situation because Eli and Mildred Carlisle had arrived to Concord, Virginia, in 1873, shortly after the Panic. They both came from Railway Money. Eli moved to Virginia because he fancied himself becoming a modern-day Thomas Jefferson—owning lots of Southern land, reading books, and thinking all the time. Since the only savings of many folks in Concord were chests full of Confederate currency (which we are still hoping will be recognized someday!) Eli and Mildred were able to buy up most everything around here. They had been sitting fat and happy up on Big Hill for several decades when Violet was born. Mildred didn't have much of a social life, as the Mary Curtis chapter of the United Daughters of the Confederacy nearly passed out, collectively, when she suggested they invite W. E. B. DuBois to one of their meetings to talk about the Plight of the Negro. As Elise MacJenkins commented, after you think a Northerner has pushed all your keys, the Yankee rolls in a brand-new piano.

Despite our initial apprehension about a learned charcoal, Violet proved not only to be sharp mentally but also smooth socially. At first, the black folk didn't quite know what to think of her, talking different from them and all. But she didn't perceive herself better than anybody. She read all the classics that Mildred would give her, but would just as soon sit at a barbecue, telling and listening to tales. The only difference was she could even write them down.

It eventually became clear to Mildred that it didn't matter how well educated Violet grew, no one was going to give her a job to do anything but clean or babysit. Mildred decided she hadn't spent years tutoring Violet so she could be a super-spelling Aunt Jemima. At Mildred's insistence, Eli started training Violet to help him with the affairs of the Carlisle estate. There were the rents, the railway bonds, the money held in Northern banks, some oil stocks, and a little land near Niagara Falls. Violet proved she could handle it all. Mildred also commented that it was savage the way Southerners kept their Negroes cooking, cleaning, caring for the children—around them all the time, like they were the family dog. She would have only a formal, professional relationship with her proof of black competence. So, to have Violet close but out of the house, they built her a little cottage in the back of Big Hill. After Mildred and Eli died, Violet helped Henry so much that he put her at the helm as he was getting older, since he reluctantly realized that his son, William, was not going to end his love affair with Jack Daniel's.

WILLIAM KEPT A CLOSE LEASH on the money Violet could use to keep up the Carlisle buildings, but he made sure that she collected all the rents on time. Often, he'd send her to pick up overdue payments from people. Despite the unpleasant nature of such a task, she managed to do it with quiet, even uplifting, grace. Eugene Wells said that when she was sent to him, she just knocked on his door and said, "You know why William has sent me here. Now, what are we going to do? I think I can hold him off for a few weeks."

She was always running around taking care of the Carlisles' business. She had some time to go to barbecues and church, but she didn't do much else. At one barbecue, though, a skinny yet striking guy from out of town told a tale about why waves have white caps, and she liked it so much, she wrote it down.

When he finished, she introduced herself to him. At twenty-three, Miles was fifteen years younger than she. When she told him she had written down the story about the waves, his eyes lit up. He wanted to learn how to write because he was filled with tales. He'd spent his early years toiling in a cotton field in South

Carolina and was attempting to move North. He asked her to teach him to write, and she told him that she'd love to, but she was really short on time.

That night, she woke up to him singing outside her window. He sang a melancholy tale about knowledge, letting people run free, and letting people go. She couldn't sleep, because he was so loud and beautiful—so finally, she just shouted, "All right, you can come in tomorrow. But you will just have to watch me read."

He was happy to. In fact, he sat right by her, making her read out loud, and after a while, he started picking up the words. She felt for him in part because, even though he was enthusiastic, his mind was tinged with the remembrances of servitude. And for the first time, she didn't feel like an experiment, but an object of love. He lived with her for about two years in the cottage in the back part of the Carlisles' land. During the pleasant evenings, on the front porch or in the living room they would often sit—telling stories. Then one day he was inspired by some words of Frederick Douglass that Violet read him, that "those who would be free, themselves must strike the first blow," so he enlisted. Violet was nervous, but he told her that he had to fight Fascism.

ABLE TO BRIDGE THE WORLD between Eugene and Miles, she grew on us all. Violet never had to sit in the back of the bus. She always had a ride. Not that Concord is big enough to have buses anyway.

Once, she was driving the Carlisles' car outside town when she spotted Elise MacJenkins broken down on the side of the road.

"Mrs. MacJenkins, you need a ride?"

Mrs. MacJenkins didn't say a word. She wasn't quite sure how she felt about talking to, much less getting in the car with, a Negro—enlightened or otherwise. But she desperately needed help. She was on an errand of mercy to slake the thirst of a bunch of dry West Virginians. If one of the Feds she had outraced came along, she'd be in serious trouble. On the other hand, if a Daughter of the Confederacy eyed her in a car with Violet, she'd have a lot of explaining to do.

"Mrs. MacJenkins, it is so hot outside, even the shadows are sweating. Now, do you need help?"

"Mmm-hmm."

"Well, let's get the moonshine out of your trunk as well."

"MILES ONCE TOLD ME WHY some people, instead of talking, say 'mmm-hmmm,'" Violet said as they drove down the road.

Elise sat silently beside her.

"When the Devil carries children away from their mommas, he puts them in his mouth. One day, he put this widow's boy in his trap and started flying off. But she ran out of her house and cried, 'Hey, Satan, you coming back for more?'

"Now, Satan is always lonely, so he always answers. And he's always hungry, so he's always coming back for more. So he said, 'You know I am!' And the moment Satan opened his mouth, that boy then fell out and ran back to his wise momma.

"So, from then on, when someone asks Satan or his minions something, they just say, 'Mmm-hmm.'"

"Mmmm-hmmm." Mrs. MacJenkins nodded as Violet pulled up to the back of her town house.

"Nice to talk to you," Violet said after she helped Elise unload her moonshine jugs.

Mrs. MacJenkins started to walk away. She then stopped and turned to Violet. "It was nice talking with you, too. Thank you for your help. Come stop by and see me sometime. I'd love to hear a few more tales. I find the best way to keep the Devil away is to share a bottle of red wine for our sweet Jesus."

"Mmm-hmm," Violet replied, and Elise laughed with her as she drove off.

"MEN, YOU ARE THE FIRST Negro tankers to ever fight in the American Army," Patton preached to Miles and his comrades of the 761st Tank Battalion. Miles stood in a drizzle at a place called St. Nicholas de Port. He thought it odd that Patton, though a General and all, didn't have the sense to put on his raincoat. But he appreciated the commander's words. "I would never have asked for you if you weren't good. I have nothing but the best in my Army. I don't care what color you are, so long as you go up there and kill those Kraut sonsabitches. Everyone has their eyes on you and is expecting great things from you. Most of all, your Race is looking forward to your success. Don't let them down, and, damn you, don't let me down!"

They didn't. The battalion cleared the way. Miles died on the outskirts of Dieuze, Germany, on November 20, 1944—right as the Allies overran the city.

They buried Miles in a Netherlands cemetery. George Patton, though, sent Violet Miles's Silver Star, along with an American flag and Purple Heart. From that day forth, she flew a flag from her porch.

Violet Graves raised her and Miles's son, James, with all the strictness and carefulness of a soldier guarding a country. She had standards to uphold, and with her son, she was going to prove again, for Mildred Ovington Carlisle, that a black can be smarter than a white. Violet taught James all she knew, and when that ran out, she asked him what he wanted to learn and taught him that, too.

And James exceeded our expectations. Part of the first integrated class at Stonewall Jackson High School, he made even Simon Donald run at full pace in the race for class rank. Impressed, Simon began talking with him after English class. One day, their conversation extended all the way to the cafeteria, and, without thinking about it, they sat down together. Florence Gay Phillips dropped her lunch tray in shock. But the friendship stuck. When they weren't feeling too competitive, they'd even help each other with homework.

WHEN LBJ SENT THE DRAFT bus to pick up the boys and take them to have their physical, Simon made sure he sat next to James. Right as the bus started off, Simon handed James a small bag of crushed herbs.

"Swallow this."

"What is it?"

"It's Jamestown-weed. I've cooked it so it won't kill you. But it will fill you with an unrecognizable, temporary craze, and you'll fail your physical."

James looked at Simon.

"Now's not the time to be playing the great American. If you don't believe me, just look at George MacJenkins. He still can't talk about his experience in the Far East."

"What about you?" James asked, offering Simon the bag.

Simon Donald crossed his legs, keeping his thighs close the

whole time. "Something tells me they're not going to like me, Jimmy."

JAMES LOOKED AT THE HERBAL gift from Simon Donald, whom he trusted. But he also thought of his father—whom he knew only from the stories his mother had told him. He pictured the American flag she flew for him. He did not take the Botanist's gift.

FOUR YEARS LATER, AFTER JAMES Graves returned from Vietnam just in time to save Simon Donald, we all had a big party for him in his front yard. The American flag fluttered where it had since 1944. Mrs. MacJenkins had made a huge pot of her liquid lightning. And we sat in the yard, drinking and laughing all night, because James Graves had gone overseas, fought, and returned.

FIVE YEARS LATER, WITHOUT MUCH of a GI Bill, James had worked his way through UVA and was looking for a job that wasn't menial labor. He and Simon Donald were on Violet's front porch, playing chess, when James all of a sudden grabbed his head.

"You all right, Jim?"

"Yeah. I'm fine." He then moved his knight.

Simon Donald, who knew himself to be terrible at chess, moved his bishop and claimed checkmate. He then looked at James. "I'm going to tell your mother that you need to see a doctor."

After weeks of hospital visits, one day Violet and James were driving back from UVA Medical Center. At three o'clock, they had not spoken a word the whole car ride home. From time to time, she just held the hand of her boy, who had three brain tumors.

AS THEY PASSED OVER THE East Concord bridge, they stopped for a moment in traffic. James looked at his momma and uttered, "Mom, you've been the best. I couldn't have asked for more. I'm not going to be a burden on you."

He was then out of the car and jumped into the October waters of the Fork River. People got out of their cars and screamed to James, but he seemed determined not to come back up.

Now, Professor Rayburn always talked about how colored people sure can run—like Jesse Owens—but they cannot swim. He hypothesized this was because Africa was so damn dry. But he didn't take into account Violet. When she ran out of her car, she didn't think twice before she jumped into the river. And when she finally came up, she had her son by the neck. She pulled him ashore, where a few people had already gathered.

Once she had dragged him out of the water, she screamed and cried, "Don't you ever say that! You have never been a burden! You are my son."

LATER, JAMES STOOD WITH SIMON in his greenhouse.

"They had us apply it to the jungle. Defoliants. To prevent hiding. We had large back sprayers and hosed out millions of gallons of the stuff."

"Do you know what the chemicals were called?"

"It came in these large drums painted with an orange stripe."

* * *

EIGHT MONTHS LATER, JAMES GRAVES lay in a hospital bed with tumors the size of golf balls trying to force their way out of his skull. Violet sat with him, holding his hand, serving him cooked peaches, his favorite other dishes, and at times, some of the tinctured moonshine that Mrs. MacJenkins kept her supplied with.

Often Simon Donald would come by and sit with them, though toward the end, James wasn't really aware of Simon. Simon really came for Violet.

"How are you holding up?"

"Okay."

"You know, Mrs. Graves, some mothers try to mold their children into who they want them to be. Others just open their hearts and minds and say, 'Run.' James once told me that you were the latter. And he appreciated that."

She pursed her lips to hold her tears back. "Even if I went through his stuff every week to make sure he stayed off the drugs?"

"Yes." Simon nodded.

ON THE THIRD OF JULY 1974, when Simon arrived at the hospital, Violet was praying before her son as the nurses turned off the machines. Simon got on his knees and prayed beside her.

"It's not fair, Simon."

"No. It's not."

"Simon, have I ever told you why waves have white caps?" Violet asked in the hospital, beside her dead son and his friend.

"No."

"The water and the wind are both mommas. The wind once

bragged to the water, 'My children are greater than yours. My birds run on the land, sail through the sky, even float across rivers and oceans. They sing pretty songs and have graceful feathers, which men admire. Your fish just swim.' The water said nothing, not even 'Mmm-hmmm.'

"The next time the wind's birdlings hopped down to the shore for water, the ocean swallowed them. The wind knows some of her missing children went to the water, and keeps calling for them there. Whenever she cries, they ruffle their feathers, saying, 'Momma! Momma! Here we are! Here we are!' But she just keeps howling so loud, she can't hear her children. Because the wind won't apologize, the water won't let the wind's birdlings go.

"We've done no bragging. Still, no matter how hard we try, they won't let our children go.

"They say it wasn't Agent Orange. Shoot, even the Devil don't lie like that, Simon. He'd at least say, 'Mmm-hmm.'"

EVERY THIRD OF JULY, THE day James passed away, you will find us assembled in the yard of Mrs. Violet Graves. On the porch is a vase of luminescent violet flowers, which Simon Donald has cut off from his famous rosebushes, as he does every year for this event. Violet Graves stands with a brand-new American flag waving before her. The two most important people in her existence risked their lives for that flag. One was killed by the Aryan man. The other found out his killer was closer to home.

Old Professor Rayburn, who did return from the trenches of the War to End All Wars, raises his bugle and plays taps.

With all the grace of Mildred Ovington Carlisle, Violet strikes a match. She then holds the flame, resolutely, under the flag. She stands there, on her swollen legs, immovable like Muzio Scevola, the great Roman who stuck his right hand into fire to show his love for his City. We remember standards, expectations, mistakes, and dreams. As the flames engulf the flag, the people of Concord, Virginia, hope to do better.

We put our flattened hands against our brows as the stripes and stars fall to ashes. And until she dismisses us, which she will with a "Thank you for being here—for Miles and James," we will not stop saluting Mrs. Violet Graves.

VI

The Botanist

"WE'D ALL BEEN DRINKING FOR some time," the twenty-two-year-old blue-eyed blond began, his jaw not completely right. "At about one thirty A.M., Jackson McCormick announced he'd had more than enough and was going to bed.

"Half an hour later, I heard some goings-on in Jackson's room. I knew he'd gone to bed pretty plastered, so I quietly opened his door and—"

"Take your time," the Prosecution encouraged.

"He was passed out and—that fairy was on him."

"How did you react?"

"I shouted, that's what I did. I said, 'What the hell is goin' on in here?' "

"And what did the boy do?"

"He jumped off the bed, against the wall. Jackson stirred from sleep. I said, 'Jackson, that faggot was sucking you off!' "

"How did Mr. McCormick react?"

"He shuddered in horror. Horror, I tell you. Disgust. 'What?' he screamed in panic."

"What did you do?"

"I grabbed the cocksucker. He yanked Jackson's wrestling trophy off the bureau behind him and hit me on top of the head. Then he threw it at Jackson and ran out the room."

"Did you go after him?"

"As Jackson helped me to my feet, we heard something falling down the stairs. When we reached them, that queer was at the bottom. A few of the guys had run out of their rooms to see what was going on. Bruised and bloody, the fairy gathered himself up and limped out of the house."

The Prosecution smugly turned to Helen Hart. "Your witness."

SIXTEEN YEARS EARLIER, ON MAIN Street in Concord, Virginia, a very young Simon Donald was in the Roses Five and Ten, looking at the spring seed packets. At the back of the store, large overhead skylights let the South's light feed the aisle's fledgling flora. Simon—enthralled by the greenery—carefully counted his change. To make the most out of his copper, nickel, and silver, he decided that he'd just buy seeds. Quickly, his paws were full of bright packets, promising a late summer of spicy tomatoes, opulent watermelons, and magical pumpkins. Still his hands reached for one more at the rack's summit.

"Excuse me, missus, will you hand me the reddish-orange flowers?" he asked Mary Anne Randolph as she wistfully walked by with her parasol in hand. Most people hadn't spoken to Mary Anne for some time, since Anne Falkland died, and no one ever asked her questions.

"Excuse me?"

"Could you help me reach those reddish-orange flowers?" He stretched his arms above his head to demonstrate his vertical challenge to the lunatic.

Mary Anne quickly grabbed the seed packet, stared intensely at it, and smiled. "Marigolds." She handed the seeds to the boy. "I plant them around my garden to keep the ants out."

"How do they do that?"

"Don't know," she realized with regret. "Aren't you one of Patricia Donald's boys?"

"Yes, ma'am."

She scanned suspiciously around herself. "You know marigolds used to be worn by the Virgin Mary. Her grace made them glow golden." Mary Anne's smile turned to a frown. "When the Indians' blood was spilled all over them, she refused to wipe it away. The stain remains on the petals' edges."

Simon continued to regard her. She thought about how it had been a long time since anyone had listened to her.

"You know if a plant is threatened, it trembles? And when you cut a flower, it cries out. But if you ever feel demons upon you, run to a flower. Hold a rosebush, and the ghosts of those who loved you will travel through the Earth, up the plant's roots, through its stems, and phoenix out of the flower to save you."

"Roses prick me." Simon pouted.

"They have to protect themselves, dear." She looked at him. "Would you like for me to teach you about flowers? I know your parents are busy with their farm, but they could probably spare you, at least until you're big enough to help out. You know my roses have won first-prize ribbons from the Garden Club of Virginia?"

Simon nodded, though he wasn't aware of the goings-on of the Garden Club. But he had a feeling he'd met a woman whom he'd be friends with for a long time.

"All right, let me talk to your momma about it."

"I HAVE FOUND PLANTS GROW best," she taught him as they placed seedlings in her garden very early one morning, "when they can talk to someone different from themselves. Tomatoes love carrots and potatoes. Squash, beans, and corn educate each other. The beds may look disorderly—but believe me, dear, a little chaos never hurt anyone. The Indians, believing it confused evil, farmed this way."

With the advice of someone whom everyone else thought was a loon, he built his own garden. By eighth grade, his flower beds held such an assortment that the Concord Bridge Club asked if they could meet among them. Simon didn't play cards, but he enjoyed listening to the wives' tales.

Once, he heard Carson Falkland ask Mrs. Elise MacJenkins why she never invited Ms. Tzigane, who owned the inn down the way, to play with the club.

"She'd probably rip up Simon's plants and use them to cast spells," the matriarch snapped.

Simon's ears pricked up. The next afternoon—with some trepidation about her exotic voice, robes, and humor—he knocked on the Blue Gypsy's door and introduced himself. She invited him in for tea, and while they were sipping, he asked if she knew anything about plants.

"Just which wild ones to eat if starving," she replied. The tips of her ears were shredded—the result, Simon suddenly realized, of someone having ripped out her earrings. She smiled a broken grin at him.

"Even around here?"

"We'll have to go wandering." She nodded.

FROM THAT DAY FORTH, ALONG the old road to town or beside the river, the two were often seen walking together with pieces of greenery in their mouths. "Sourwood leaves are my favorite." Simon laughed with her one late summer day as they stood underneath a tree, sucking its foliage.

"GHOSTS LIVE IN ALL THINGS," Mary Anne Randolph had taught, planting within him the seeds of curiosity. In school, he studied in a possessed fashion. When the Supreme Court integrated the previously all-white high school, Simon remembered Mary Anne had told him that fruits and vegetables grow best when they can talk with someone different from themselves. So, he started talking to the smart, black James Graves after an English class on *Leaves of Grass.*

It was James's willingness to say what everyone knew but people feared saying that Simon admired. Oblivious of the risks and controversy involved, Simon started eating lunch with James. He then introduced him to Lily and Betty Joe, who—as beautiful, clever women—ran the social order of their grade.

Simon snapped up the Robert E. Lee Scholarship to attend Jefferson College, a privilege the school awarded annually to let a local boy get his letters amongst his betters. James, commenting that his cheeks were beyond the pale for such an award, went to Vietnam.

* * *

"MR. GILLIAM, HOW LONG HAVE you known Jackson McCormick?" Helen Hart, the Defense attorney, asked.

"We both pledged Kappa Alpha our sophomore year, so over three years."

"And he's spent most of his evenings at the Kappa Alpha House?"

"Jackson? Naw. He spent a lot of nights out."

"Where?"

"With one of the girls from Hollins or Mary Baldwin, I guess."

The Judge on the bench looked as if Jefferson Davis had appointed him before the Yankees so impolitely stormed into Richmond. He seemed proud of the cobwebs he'd earned by staying in the same place for so long.

"Mr. Gilliam, I know that you must have had the utmost concern for Jackson McCormick when you entered his room, but, out of curiosity, how would you have reacted if Jackson had been awake when you saw him with Mr. Donald?"

Alex Gilliam hesitated.

"Objection, the witness cannot be expected to describe what he may or may not have done."

"Sustained."

"JACKSON MCCORMICK," THE PROSECUTION ASKED after the man swore to tell the truth, "how did you meet Simon Donald?"

"We were freshman-year roommates."

"Were you close?"

"We got along okay. He spent most of his time in the library."

"What happened after that freshman year?"

"Well, I moved into the KA House and Simon stayed in the dorms."

"Did you remain friends?"

"We saw each other around. If KA was having a party, I'd tell him to swing by. I sort of felt for the little fellow. There's no excuse for what he did to me."

HELEN HART ROSE. "MR. MCCORMICK, was the night of April sixteenth your only sexual encounter with another man?"

"Yes, ma'am."

"And over the past few years, you've spent several nights a week away from the frat house with young ladies at nearby colleges? Is that true?"

"Yes."

"How did you stay the evening with them?"

"What?"

"No respectable women's college allows men in the dorms after dark. So, where did you stay?"

"The Roanoke Inn and, in Staunton, the Woodrow Wilson House."

"Staunton is only thirty miles from Concord. Why didn't you just drive home?"

"The girls all wanted to be with me and had to be back in the dorms early."

"Can you give us the names of these young ladies so that they might explain to the court how they were able to evade *in loco parentis*?"

"Objection. The court cannot expect a well-bred young lady to testify under the eyes of the Commonwealth that she has acted with impropriety."

"Such women have something to fear only if the Commonwealth starts sending people to jail for acting with what it believes is impiety," Helen pointedly replied.

"Overruled," the Judge agreed.

Jackson paused. "It would bring dishonor to the names of the young ladies, so I must respectfully say I can't remember."

"Had Simon Donald—in all the time he knew you—ever expressed his physical or romantic interest in men?"

"He was always talking about his friend Jimmy Graves, but that's about it."

"Have you ever been in love, Mr. McCormick?"

Jackson glared at Helen.

"Objection, Your Honor, such a personal question has no bearing—," the Prosecution broke in.

"The Prosecution seeks to send the defendant to a decade of prison for an alleged personal act. Surely his accuser can answer this simple question."

"I will allow it." The Judge, when not lost in joyous reverie for the cotillions of his youth, seemed amused by Helen's logic.

"Love is when you're always there for someone, no matter what," Jackson's strong-boned face stated. "So, I guess not yet."

"DO THEY HAVE ANY WITNESSES besides the pansy?" Jackson's father, a Charleston shipping magnate, asked the Prosecution attorney as they sucked Cuban cigars in the men's room during a recess.

Old Professor Rayburn was having a slow time peeing a few urinals down from them.

"Just that crazy lady. They also have some colored man on the list, but they're not sure if he'll show."

"A coon as a character witness in Richmond?" Jackson's father derided.

"Women lawyers."

"DAD, LET'S DROP THIS," JACKSON requested as they washed their hands.

Old Professor Rayburn was still having a slow time peeing.

"Hell no, son. You'll be Senator one day. Jefferson College didn't set the record straight, but the Commonwealth of Virginia will—or I'll have the Governor and the whole House of Burgesses whipped."

HELEN HART LOOKED NERVOUS AS Mary Anne Randolph—in a green dress—timidly stepped into the witness box.

"Ms. Randolph, can you please describe what happened last April sixteenth?"

She slowly began. "I was on one of my late-night drives when I felt some commotion occurring in the yard of the Kappa Alpha House."

"What do you mean by 'felt'?"

"I heard it, but I also felt it in my skin. The air smelled of violation. The trees howled with alarm!"

"And what did you do?"

"I stopped, grabbed my shovel out of the backseat, and ran to see what was going on—"

"And what was going on?"

"There must have been at least a dozen of them, all in a heathen circle, kicking Simon from one side to the other like he was one of those big white mushroom balls that pop up in the spring or an Indian caught stealing food! He was holding his back, and as I ran toward him, he fell on the ground. Then, with death in their laughter, they stormed in on him."

She became possessed. "Heyenwatha! Atatarho! With my shovel, I smote a man. Then I took phalanx formation over Simon. Then that fellow over there"—she pointed to Alex Gilliam—"moved forward with a big stick to hurt us, so I whammed him on the face with my shovel. Ha! And then the other boys—all around—started throwing stones and sticks. But I beat them off! Ah! Ah! Ah! And then I started to fume, fume because they kept on around me. So the Ghosts started rising up! Owenheghkohna!

"They ran, taking with them the boys I hit. And I picked up Simon and drove him to the hospital."

"Thank you, Ms. Randolph."

Mary Anne began to step down from the box.

"Not so fast, Ms. Randolph," the Prosecution snipped. "I have a few questions for you."

Mary Anne looked nervously toward Helen Hart, who gave her a reassuring glance.

"Ms. Randolph, how do you know Simon Donald?"

"I taught him about vegetables."

"What did you teach him?"

"How to talk to them."

"Who?"

"The plants."

The Prosecution rolled his eyes. A juror laughed.

"Why did you have a shovel in your car?"

"I always keep a shovel in my backseat."

"Why?"

"You never know when you're going to have to dig something up."

The jurors now looked worried.

"Ms. Randolph, don't you find it strange that, according to your story—you, a very pale woman well past your debutante days—beat off a dozen strapping young men with just a shovel?"

Very confused, she shrugged her white eyebrows.

"Don't worry about it, Ms. Randolph. No further questions."

THE DEFENSE CALLED SIMON DONALD to the stand.

Old Lady MacJenkins, sitting in the audience, shuddered when she saw Simon. Now that she knew what she had always known about him—but hadn't acknowledged to herself that she knew—she wasn't quite sure what she should or should not think of him or his flowers, let alone the bridge games played among them. "He looks wilted," she whispered to Alistair MacGregor, who sat beside her.

"Simon Donald, the Prosecution has charged you with forcing sodomy on April sixteenth of this year. Why do you plead not guilty?"

"Because Jackson McCormick and I had been lovers for almost four years."

Jackson's father laughed.

"When and how did this start?"

Simon lowered his eyes. "In the fall of our freshman year. One night we'd been drinking at a party, and we stumbled home together. After we got to our room and climbed into our beds, we began to do what guys do before they fall asleep.

"But that night I decided to acknowledge what we both knew we did with the other listening, every evening. So—continuing—I went over to his bed, very slowly, and I climbed in with him."

"Did you force him?"

"He never said stop—or no."

"You then began to sleep together?"

"Yes. Often, he'd go off to a dance with a girl, rub up on her all night. I might join him on a double date and just be friendly. Then, at the end of the evening, we'd come back to the room and make love."

"Make love?"

"He always held me. Eventually we started to kiss. Sometimes, he wept."

"And did these encounters continue after that freshman year?"

"He would often come to my dorm room after dark, and we'd study together and then go to bed. In the morning, we often ran along the Chessie tracks."

"What happened the evening of April sixteenth?"

"Both drunk, we decided to stay in his room. We'd done it a few times before, but we forgot to lock the door this time."

"What occurred when Alex Gilliam walked in on you?"

"When he grabbed me, I squirmed, snatched a trophy off the bureau behind me, and knocked Alex upside the head with it. Jackson was screaming at me, so I hurled it at him and ran."

"Did you fall down the stairs and injure yourself?"

"No. I ran clean out the front door, thought I was in the clear. Then a rock hit me in the head. Suddenly a gang was around me."

SIMON REMEMBERED ANGRY VOICES.

"Come on, Jack, hit the little homo."

Jackson McCormick stood still. "That's enough. We've gone too far."

"Think of what he was doing to you!"

Simon couldn't breathe. Someone slammed him on his back, making it feel like his kidney broke open. He fell onto the ground. Another man moved forward and kicked him on the side of his head, slightly ripping his ear.

Jackson looked at his frat brothers, who were staring at him and wondering why he wasn't reveling in the fun. He wanted to pick up Simon, pick him up and run fast and far away.

He walked up to Simon, thinking he would indeed pick him up and run. But for some reason—oh God, he doesn't know why—he just started kicking, kicking, kicking. He wasn't going to stop, couldn't stop now, not until he was finished. He'd blot out the record of his invisible life. Wash all away. Simon shouldn't have started it in the first place.

"Yeah! Beat the fuck out of the faggot!"

"AND?" HELEN ASKED.

"Jackson joined in." And after that phrase, Simon wept.

"Can you be more specific?"

Simon didn't answer.

"Can you please be more specific, Mr. Donald?"

"They were laughing. It didn't feel like he was going to stop. I forced myself up and tried to get away, but I stumbled again at a dogwood. I grabbed its trunk and prayed.

"And then I heard a banshee—calling forth dead Indian warriors."

A COUPLE OF WOMEN IN the jury whispered to each other as they squinted at Simon suspiciously. One man stared at Simon as if he smelled funny. The Prosecution remarked that Simon Donald, like all homosexuals, was delusional. The Judge asked if there were any more witnesses. A courier carried into the room a note with a large envelope and handed it to Helen. She read the note and nodded.

"The Defense calls Sergeant James Graves—and welcomes him home from Vietnam."

He might have been black, clean shaven, and with cropped hair—but it was almost like Jesus himself walked through those heart-pine doors. He was a coon, all right—black as night. This knight had the shoulders and waist that come only after a zillion chin-ups, push-ups, and crunches. Simon, surprised, smiled when he saw his old friend dressed in full uniform. Jackson quacked when he saw the man taking the stand.

Answering Helen's questions, Sergeant Graves explained how Simon and he had become friends.

"Sergeant Graves," Helen asked, "have you ever had a homosexual experience with anyone—particularly anyone in this room?"

He paused. "You know I can get in a lot of trouble for saying what I'm about to say, but yes. One man. I have known him." He pointed at Jackson.

The gray-eyebrowed Judge leaned forward. Suddenly, he vaguely remembered in the labyrinth of his misty mind that President Thomas Jefferson decided death was indeed a too-harsh punishment for sodomy. But what would Jefferson have thought of sodomy with a black person? That is—one who wasn't a slave?

"That man? Can you tell us his name?" Helen asked.

"He didn't give me his name when I met him, or his real name, but that's him in the front row all right."

"And in what sense have you known him?"

"In the biblical sense, ma'am."

The courtroom gasped. Mrs. MacJenkins opened a jar of moonshine and passed it down her bench for people to take a few nips off of.

"Could you please be more specific, Sergeant Graves?"

"He performed oral sex on me."

Jackson's mother leaned over and asked his father what that meant. He elbowed her to silence.

"You're sure?" Helen asked.

"Yes, ma'am. I've been to Asia and back and never had a blow job done that well."

"Objection! The court cannot be expected to listen to this filth from a nigger friend of the defendant," the Prosecution roared.

"Sergeant Graves has served the Armed Forces for four years with distinction. Surely the Court—"

The Judge nodded, a tear forming in his eye as he thought of his days in the Cavalry.

"Whether or not Sergeant Graves had sexual relations with Mr. McCormick has no bearing on whether or not Mr. McCormick was violated by Simon Donald."

"Jackson McCormick has testified under oath that he's had no homosexual experiences except for the night a fraternity brother caught him with the defendant. This is relevant to his credibility as well as his—"

"Yes, yes. The witness may proceed."

"I also brought photos." James pointed to the large envelope resting on the Defense table.

"Your Honor," the Prosecution begged, "I move for a recess. I have not had an opportunity to examine the—"

For many decades, the Judge had thought that he might die within the hour, and he had little patience for attempts to delay his eminent proceedings—especially now that something stimulating was finally happening after all these years. "Let the witness finish testifying, then I will give you all the recess you want!"

With that, Helen Hart held up a huge photograph of Jackson McCormick, mouth stretched, in an attempt to swallow a black cucumber. Despite the effort involved, McCormick did not appear under duress. Somehow, he even managed a grin.

One juror covered her eyes. Another put on his glasses. Mary Anne Randolph took a gander at Jackson's father, who had turned a deep red, reminding her that her sugar beets would be ready in a few weeks.

"Objection!"

"The witness did not inform me until a few moments ago that he was willing to testify, and so I was unable to submit these beforehand." She held up another for the Jury, this one with Jackson's eyes enraptured.

"Clearly Mr. McCormick was not sleeping through this experience," Helen stated to the Jury. "When were these taken, Sergeant Graves?"

"Earlier this week. He was smoking a cigarette outside a bar in Staunton, and I asked him for a light. He took me inside, bought me a drink, and then asked if I'd like to spend the evening with him."

"What did you say?"

"I recommended a small inn on the outskirts of Concord. The proprietress, a Blue Gypsy, ended up being quite a voyeur and eavesdropper. She even made a tape." And with that, he reached inside his coat pocket and handed Helen a cassette.

Helen slipped a player out of her briefcase and put it on the Defense table.

"Judge, I was not made aware of this evidence either!" The

Prosecution was on the brink of breakdown. Jackson, sweating almost as much as he had in his first encounter with James, buried his head in his arms. Behind him, his mother opened her purse and started popping opiates. His father, shocked numb, listlessly opened his palm. She obediently gave him the rest to down.

"The Prosecution was made well aware of the witness, whom he has referred to disparagingly, and simply underestimated his capabilities."

"In more ways than one." The Judge gawked at the photos. "Overruled."

Helen hit PLAY, and the courtroom was filled with a voice that, even though heaving and panting, clearly echoed the man who had taken the stand earlier that day to accuse. When Jackson moaned, "Stick it in," a juror fainted. The voice of Sergeant Graves said, "No. I can't do this," yet still Jackson begged for it.

"Let the court record note that there is audio and visual evidence of a Mr. Jackson McCormick enthusiastically and forcefully indulging in sodomy on a significant Negro penis," the Judge ruled.

"Something tells me he's not going to be able to run for Senator!" Professor Rayburn, hard of hearing, shouted to Ms. Stetson. She was mentally planning the front page for her paper. "I wonder if I can use those photos," she asked herself, loudly enough for everyone to hear.

THE PROSECUTION, ON HEARING PROFESSOR Rayburn and Ms. Stetson, leered at Jackson McCormick in disgust. "Your Honor, the Commonwealth would like to drop charges against Mr. Simon Donald."

The people from Concord, all sitting on the side of the Defense, stood up and cheered! The other side sat dumb. "You are no longer our son," Jackson's father and mother coldly hissed behind him. Turning their backs on him for good, they swept out of the courtroom.

James hopped off the stand and hugged his botanist friend, who was crying in exuberance. He hitched his arm akimbo to Simon's. Then, with Helen grinning in front, they ambulated out of the court amidst our standing applause. If we'd had flower petals, we would have thrown them.

Mrs. MacJenkins commented that she still didn't quite know what to think of Simon Donald. He sure did mix up the normal order around Concord, Virginia. But it was best to acknowledge and not hide what we all knew we knew, yet didn't want to say that we knew—even if it was a little confusing at times. As Mary Anne Randolph taught, a little chaos is good for growth. It also keeps the evil spirits at bay.

ONCE THEY HAD REACHED THE outside, Simon turned to James and slapped him on the cheek. "That's for letting him do something I've been dying to do for years."

Simon then smiled at his dear friend—as different from him as a butternut tree is from a marigold—and opened his arms. "And here's a thank-you for rescuing me, no matter what."

James grinned, picked laughing Simon up, and twirled him around.

VII

The Builders

WHAT ARE YOU DOING TO me?"

THEY CHAINED HIM TO A formation called the Natural Bridge, a wonder of the world. Made from Ordovician limestone, it spans ninety feet from one cliff to the next, twenty stories above the Fork River in the Concord Pass. The structure is just wide enough for ten people to walk across holding hands. Geologists say water created the formation by whittling its way through the side of a mountain. People in these parts, though, reckon it's more likely just a miracle of God. At sunset, before the great arch, we have a light show, inaugurated by President Coolidge, called the Drama of Creation.

Now it is the day after Christmas, and the tourists who usually flock to this outdoor temple are all home cleaning. Instead of sightseers, this place is visited by members of the Klan. Their robes camouflage them with the landscape, which also has been sheeted by white. So, it is with a feeling of anonymity that they chain Tom Dorian to the top of our Bridge of the Great Spirit.

BLACK AS INK, TOM DORIAN is the new husband of Dahlia Wells, a redheaded girl who might be from a family of trash, but is still white. No matter that Tom Dorian is the best carpenter in town (and has successfully out-bid and -performed his rivals on more than one contract job), the men who bound him to this eroded mountain on this morning were absolute in their conviction that he was subhuman. As he screamed and grappled with them, they bound his hands and legs with hemp cord. After wrapping the chain around his thighs and waist, they brought it under the Bridge and back to him, where they padlocked the links together. Once winter had murdered him, the Klan members thought, they could convey him around to the Bridge's belly and leave him for tourists to find. Perhaps they could just dangle him in the archway between cliffs, as greetings for times to come. Or, they would just leave him, on top of the Bridge, for no one to find.

"Let me go." Tom asked.

THE DRAPED MEN, CHECKING THAT he was firmly bound, slowly backed away.

ON THE NATURAL BRIDGE, TOM thought of his Dahlia. He reminisced about swimming with her on his rare days off in Lime Creek. Of all places, she would not think of looking for him here. He would need to hope for another love, from another time, a woman who could find him even when he was invisible. But would she remember?

He watched the copper sunset. Castor and Pollux rose in the clear winter sky, so dark and only heaven-lit, he felt—if it weren't for the chains—he could have fallen, fallen upward into the stars and disappeared forever. He was alone here, he knew, and no one would be able to find him.

"Mockingbird, will you please keep quiet?" he begged as he woke the next morning. The long-tailed gray bird perched on the top of a nearby crag shaped like a balled-up fist. Strangely, the bird's song was not recognizable as that of cardinal, purple martin, raven, or any of the other local birds of the area, Tom thought. No. It sang a strange song, which carried through the cold wind effortlessly and even echoed within Tom's Negro chest. Its sure voice seemed as though it might transmit even to the top of faraway Deadman Mountain.

And as Tom slept, he had a dream. A vision from long ago, before even the white oaks and twisted bonsai-like pines that are now on the Bridge were seedlings. Yet there were others, much the same, but in different places. . . .

A BROWN TURKEY BUZZARD LANDED ten feet from Tom, waking him. On the other side, a black vulture landed, too. The buzzard and the vulture glared at each other, claiming the dark meat as their own. Tom attempted to raise his torso and swing around his bound hands. The carrion feeders did not sway but poised to start their repast early.

The mockingbird blessed her song with hissing and alighted onto the chains around Tom's waist. The wind answered with a howl. A frozen branch from a nearby white oak cracked off and nearly cold-cocked the buzzard. In fear, it took to the air. The black vulture, opening its silent mouth to the mockingbird, then fled also.

"Mockingbird, keep singing." Tom smiled and nodded. He then thanked heaven as he listened to that white-patched gray bird perched on his chains. And, despite the bonds against his waist, peace graced his heart as the animal called out a lullaby.

DARKNESS CAME. ORION, WITH HIS bright belt, was what he saw, for the clouds had covered the Twins. He could make out the seven sister Pleiades, and of course, the Northern Star. As Tom drifted, his eyes opened from time to time, each wakening focusing on that star of freedom at the end of the Little Bear. He'd see the constellations circularly around the stable star, whose mythical power he wanted to carry into his reality. He'd also listen for the mockingbird, who would always be there, within earshot. In a way, the music sounded like the spirituals his mother had taught him, or one of the ones he'd heard from Violet Graves.

Toward the end of evening, he knew the caller would not abandon him—and he fell into a deep sleep.

ONE HEADLIGHT. A QUIETLY CLOSING wooden door of an over-a-decade-old wood-bodied station wagon. Worried but guided footsteps. A cotton dress tearing on a dormant blackberry vine. Closer. Closer.

"Hello out there. Hello! Is there someone who can hear me?" she called into the indigo air.

"Hello! Here! Can you hear me? Over here," the male voice replied.

Stumbling through the bramble was a forty-something-year-old woman, about his age, with hair perfectly bobbed at the chin and nails closely clipped to allow easy piano playing. She wore a long white shawl over a plain navy blue cotton dress and old brown boots. Despite all the efforts to appear perfectly normal, something could not be mistaken. Her hair, her eyebrows, everything except her sunglass-covered eyes—was stark white.

Around her flew the harsh *chack*ing mockingbird.

"I'm here. Hold on." Fearful of the large drop on either side, Mary Anne Randolph tentatively stepped onto the Bridge and upon Thomas. Pink dawn cast over them.

A voice within Tom spoke, yet it was another man's speech. "Shhh—He's sleeping."

"Then how is he or you or whomever talking to me?" she puzzled with fear.

"He's fallen into a deep sleep, from which it would be better for him not to wake, so I have come to speak to you from his body in his stead. Don't ask me how he could have fallen asleep, especially with the incessant *chack* of that mockingbird."

"The Klan did this. I think they were the ones who knocked out one of my headlights. They think it's strange that I always go on late-night drives." Mary Anne took off her large rose-tinted sunglasses and peered at Thomas with her red eyes.

"Do you know who I am, Mary Anne?" the voice within Tom asked.

"How is it that I hear people long since gone? And sometimes, when people speak, I hear the names of the dead. And your soul—"

"I live on only in you, a descendant, and Tom Dorian here—"

"The Bible tells us that Jesus rose from the—"

"The Bible tells us that Joshua saw the sun stand still for several hours. A body, revolving on its axis, stopped. Should that sudden stoppage not have laid flat all the animals, buildings, and done the same when it started up again? Does that, like the miracles of Jesus, sound within the realm of possibilities?"

"Sort of like all men are created equal," she shyly countered.

With his wide dark eyes, Tom looked around. Perched on the rocks and the trees of the Bridge were a cardinal, purple martin, raven, robin, blue jay, oriole, sparrow, phoebe, horned lark, meadowlark, yellow warbler, and the mockingbird. "What are we arguing about?"

"The past."

"I like the dreams of the future better. Let Tom go."

"Yes, yes. Of course." Mary Anne crouched and crawled to Tom to inspect the lock.

"Oh, woman, this is in vain. Even Heracles could not break these chains. You better go to town and find the strongest Negro you can and tell him to bring tools."

Fumbling with the links, Mary Anne touched Thomas. Suddenly, she was sharing a memory with the guest spirit within him.

THEY'RE IN THE NIGHT. WATER giggles and hums around rocks. Huge sycamore trees stretch up to the heavens and reach out over the river, like they want to dip their branches into the water. The third-quarter moon rises within the victory arch of the large Natural Bridge. A brand-new wood-bodied station wagon pulls onto the side of the road. A pale face walks down the rock steps. At the river's edge, she slips off her maroon dress and hangs it on a branch. Despite the moon's only dim light, there's no mistaking her bleach-white skin. She dips into the river's pool.

"Ma'am. I'm in the water, too. I don't want to frighten you, but I'm swimming, too," a strong male says.

"What are you doing here at this hour?" Mary Anne replies, curiously not scared.

"Swimming, like you, ma'am."

"I mean, what are you doing swimming now? It's a half hour before midnight."

"I could ask the same of you."

"Well, when else is a girl like me supposed to be able to swim in the open air and not get burned?"

"I don't—"

"I'm Mary Anne Randolph."

"The albino?"

"Don't rub it in. I have sensitive skin." She swims closer to the voice, which she recognizes. She feels she is right before him. "God, you're dark."

"That's a rock, ma'am. I'm over here."

Mary Anne turns around and sees the whites of his eyes. She then swims within a few feet of him. "Ah! Tom Dorian. Almost invisible. What brings you to the Concord Pass at this hour?"

"I just got off work."

"Really? You work too hard."

"Not much choice, ma'am."

"Right. Well, why are you swimming here?"

"Colored folks aren't allowed on tours of the Bridge. At this hour, though, I can hide in its shadows. You?"

"Hiding, too. And I feel connected to the Bridge because it belonged to my ancestor. And my momma, after she moved to the sticks of Concord from New Orleans, commented that the archway was the most sublime of sights."

"It sure does make pretty cover." Tom smiles.

Something skims the water between them.

"Well, I won't tell anyone about you if you don't tell anyone about me. People already think I'm a loon."

"You have a deal."

"Besides, it will be nice to have someone to keep me company out here in the water at this hour. Anne Falkland used to come out here with me at twilight, before she—you know—last winter. Perhaps we can play swimming tag or something—"

"Yeah. And keep an eye out for things. I'm always scared of turtles or snakes."

With her pale hand, she reaches out of the dark pool and taps him on the shoulder. "You're it."

She then swims, with graceful power, freestyle away from him and the archway. He counts to three and follows.

IN SOFT YELLOW DAYLIGHT, MARY Anne Randolph was pulling away from Tom, who was chained to the rock bridge.

She grabbed a large square gray stone. Eyes welling up, she placed it on his feet.

"What are you—? Did you not have a courtship of night swimming with this Negro Tom Dorian—one summer in your youth?" the aristocratic voice within dark skin asked.

"A friendship. With propriety. And with someone who thought it was perfectly normal to be more comfortable in the dark.

"That summer was great for night swimming because every day it grew so muggy, the sky just about exploded with thunderstorm around three or four in the afternoon. So, all those normal people would often stay at home. What is the point of making a trip to the river if you might get struck by lightning, like Elise's son? But the rains just lasted for about thirty minutes or so. That's all. The landscape was lush—like the rain forests Ms. Stetson wrote about visiting, so there was no muddy runoff. A summer of clear, fresh water—that became covered by moon mirrors—celebrated by the loose banjo songs of the green frogs, the deep bellows of the bullfrogs, and our whispers.

"And, of course, the fireflies, which rose over the water and the wood around us. We would often talk about what they reminded us of. Sparks and crackles in the silver screen we were in. Countless camera flashes. Like the stars were being born. As they rose to space, you were not quite sure where Earth stopped and Heaven began. The glowing bodies were especially bright as they flew against silhouetted Earth forms that were without a third dimension—so they appeared as high as you wanted them to be.

"In the night, you don't want to get out of the river, because the air is colder than the water. And, even though bats constantly skim and fleck the river with their hand-wings, there are mosquitoes that the water protects one from. I told Tom this, and a few days later, when I arrived to the river, he'd hung a huge mosquito net from one of the great sycamore branches. The net draped over a large sandstone rock and part of the water. I thanked him, and he laughed and said he'd done it for himself. 'The bugs like me because I'm so sweet.' He shrugged. 'And I got sensitive skin.' Even though we had that net to rest under, we still spent most of our time swimming upstream and drifting back down, under the Bridge.

"Sometimes, we'd sit on the rock with the wide net above and drop a hook in the water. Usually, we'd catch a shiny brook trout. Since we didn't want to light a fire under our safe mosquito net, we'd slice the fish open, debone it, and, with salt and vinegar—eat it raw. Toward late July, we'd garnish it with a spicy tomato from my garden.

"Once, he met me right as I was leaving my automobile and told me to be very quiet. We then slowly swam to the pool under the Bridge. There, courting on the small walkway, was a pair of black-crowned night herons. We drifted within a few feet from them, yet they didn't detect us at all. But even at the hour after my death, I will remember their night music and dance—clapping of bills, flapping of wings, cocking of heads to the shadowy vault of the Bridge.

"For me, it was a summer of silver. For in those two and a half months, I saw a thousand different shades of silver, cast by the heavens—over the water, the Natural Bridge, and our bodies. Sometimes faint. Sometimes tinged with blue. Green—because of the trees. Silver orange. Yellow, for the fireflies.

"All summer, a songbird roosted in the branch above our net. We couldn't figure out what it was, because its song was sometimes close to that of a blue jay and other times an oriole or robin—we lost track of how many birds we'd guessed. Perhaps a lot of birds were up there after all. Then, the last night, Tom sang to me a spiritual, and the bird whistled it back. We then realized that it was a mockingbird. Laughing, we let ourselves go. Though we were careful, well, I guess you can only be so careful in the water.

"The color between black and white is not what people think.

"The color between Tom and me was silver, like the moon and the constellations—which we learned together one by one that season. And I believed that it was through the heavens that I had conceived, and the baby would be silver. No matter what, I figured that the child would be fine. I'm too white. Tom was too black. The baby would be just right for American society. But my father didn't agree. An heir of Jefferson having a black baby? He would not have it."

* * *

MARY ANNE PICKED UP A large flat piece of shale. The birds, in agreement, followed her with their eyes as she dragged the stone over to Thomas and laid it across his shins.

"What are you doing with these rocks?"

"I'm making sure your soul will never be able to get off this rock bridge. If Tom Dorian dies chained here before sunset, these stones will keep your soul bound to the Bridge forever."

She walked away, brushing her pale gloves together.

"The animosity after slavery will always be too great. Reconciliation between black and white is beyond the realm of possibilities. Only deportation would have solved the Negro problem. You should know at least that."

"Stop talking down to me. Belittling destroys hope."

"You're just a sensitive—"

The birds flew around Mary Anne and then settled in new places.

"It's fine for me to be sensitive." Mary Anne grabbed his bound hands. "Fleeing my daddy, I moved to New Orleans, played piano for the Hotel Monteleon, and lived with my momma's family, believing my baby would be silver. Then one night I was out alone walking in the French Quarter, down Royal Street, and came across the Pirate's Alley. I ambled down it because it is such a delightful little place. Then, out of nowhere, a black man flashed his steel knife at me.... His eyes were fearful, without hope.

"The baby was stillborn a day later. Black, with reddish hair.

"Years later, Tom invited me to his and Dahlia's wedding." She released her grasp on him. "Never have I been so jealous of white trash. But look, the Klan has gone wild even over that marriage.

Can you imagine what they would have done in response to mine?"

"He likes redheads. And who can blame him? I was even known to turn a few heads in my day with a tussle of my hair," Thomas replied.

The cardinal sang out a *sweet-sweet-sweet-sweet.*

Mary Anne picked up a rock that looked like a twisted piece of petrified wood, three feet long. She dragged it over to Thomas and laid it across his thighs.

"This rock looks like a branch," he commented.

"Blanche was the name of my momma, who, too, was a haunted albino—and who died giving birth to me."

The sun colored the landscape orange.

"My soul is going to be fine. I just can't believe you're going to let this black man die on this rock!"

"One for the auction block."

"All I wanted for Virginia was for it to aspire to the dream landscape it is—and to love the earth."

"A serene pastoral scene of lazy white farmer sitting on porches telling niggers how to dig in the dirt," she hissed.

A storm rose near them. A blanket of ashy winter clouds floated above the lowering sun.

"All my wishes end, where I hoped my days would end. It could exist only by slaves slaving from dawn to dusk."

"All you had to do was lift your famed pen to make it okay for me to love Tom Dorian," she spoke back.

The purple martin sent out a penetrating *tee-tee-tee.*

"Mourn. Show your hope and faith in humankind. It would have been a lot easier than my picking up this rock." Mary Anne lifted up a large green-and-black rock, nelsonite.

"I am dying, Virginia, dying."

"Virginia was the name of my black daughter, who was born dead shortly after I was robbed by that nigger."

"It was not my folly."

"Molly was the name of my foremother, who was kidnapped by the Shawnees after they lost hope." She lowered the rock down on his hip.

"Mary Anne, stop blaming me. We did our best given the place and times. You are not the only one who had to keep a lover secret."

The raven began a deep guttural croaking, a wooden *wonk-wonk*.

"I had a staircase, a narrow twisting staircase that went from my study right down, below, to Sally's chamber. And almost every night I was home at Monticello, she would come to me—or sometimes I would descend into her quarters to her. In the evening, the Declaration, the Statute, the University brought no comfort. Without Sally, I was alone in bed and in dream. Even in summer, the sheets were invariably too cold.

"Yes, I have to admit that the only thing that made me feel healthy and alive for decades was a quarteroon. For some time, I thought I could do what I did with her because she wasn't that black. But no. It was because, like you, I found that only silver exists among two lovers in the dark."

"The Hemmings—?"

"I have never denied it. Indeed, how do you think I speak to you now? Isaac, meet your Ishmael."

"I'm related to that Negro? But we had an affair!"

"Mary Anne, I wouldn't worry about it. In my day, people slept with first and second cousins all the time."

In the red light, Mary Anne covered her face.

"Granted, it would explain what happened to the royals, wouldn't it?"

"Did you love her?"

He lowered his jaw, inquisitively, and lifted his eyebrows. "I loved women of intellect, culture beyond even my own."

"Did you love her?"

"Her beauty gave me peace in my grandest years." He panned his upward facing palm through the air.

"Did you love her?"

"I loved my wife, Martha." He spoke firmly. "If I loved Sally at all, it was because she, too, was John Wayles's daughter, even if it was by a mulatto. Sally was my wife's dark sister, the changeling left after an early death."

Mary Anne sat on the Bridge. "To make love to someone over time and not feel for them. It is something that I don't think is possible for a woman. Be it biology or not, a woman will feel love or disgust, but she will feel."

"Mary Anne." The sun neared setting. Thomas reached over and gently touched Mary Anne with his tied hands. She was numb. Seeing her distraction, he suddenly swung his arms over her head, holding her to his chest. "Untie Tom's hands. Just untie his hands and perhaps he will be able to do the rest. You can do at least that!"

Without nails to claw him with, Mary Anne forced Thomas's arms up and sunk her teeth into one of them. He screamed. Like an angry falcon, she bit harder until he ripped his arms away back over her head.

"Don't you see?" he shouted. "All this is for nothing. Except, here on this Virginian rock, a Negro is going to die.

"My soul carries no debts. The dead inherit nothing. We are

like limestones that break under iron chains. Your rocks have no power."

Mary Anne scrambled away. Under a scraggly Virginia pine, she picked up a globe-sized dark limestone veined with calcium. The sun reached the top of Deadman Mountain. The cheerful birds circled her in flight, like a school of fish, yet of multiple patterns. They made their own calls as she hauled up the spherical rock. From the teeth gashes Mary Anne had made, Thomas's blood ran down his arm. The mockingbird alighted on his chains again and sent out harsh *chack*s. Thomas took to his mouth the gash to stop the bleeding.

The mockingbird kept chanting. The cardinal, purple martin, raven, and other birds all started circling both Mary Anne and Thomas. And as he tasted the blood of Tom Dorian, the birds' spirituals and flight became a story. A woman watching an old man descend a spiral staircase . . . a voice that possessed but did not love . . . a turning of the back for paradise . . .

"His justice will not sleep forever," he heard the mockingbird sing. All the other birds were now silent, though still flying around the two of them.

"Mary Anne, you are right! Do not let me be bound here forever. He will not be able to make it through the night. The sun is falling behind the mountain."

Mary Anne cradled the globe-sized stone in her arms, like a baby, toward Thomas.

"Forgive me. I knew not what I was doing!" he cried out.

"You have to make your decision, Mary Anne," decreed the mockingbird. The black vulture and the buzzard had returned, each circling high in the sky. Only a quarter of the sun remained above Deadman Mountain. Feeling his doom had arrived, Thomas closed his eyes. Mary Anne heaved the heavy white-and-dark-blue stone above her head.

AND DARKNESS DID NOT HAPPEN. When Thomas opened his eyes, the sun had not yet set. Instead, a crescent just sat there, above the mountain, suspended in time. Its white-gold rays beamed through the landscape, illuminating Mary Anne's red eyes, white skin, and blue dress.

Thomas stared at the sun. He gasped. A few steps from them stood three members of the Klan. Two held lit torches. The other stepped forward, pointing a silver engraved French pinfire revolver.

"Let us be," Mary Anne ordered.

They staggered toward her.

"I said let us be!"

The birds landed on or beside her, as guards against the cloaked men. The buzzard and vulture hissed.

Two cloaked men raised their torches. The other cocked his pistol. Mary Anne gazed knowingly at the engraved gun and then into the ghouls' eyes.

"There are no secrets in Concord," she warned.

The birds opened their wings, greeting a gale that extinguished the flames.

The men bowed and backed away.

"That's impossible." Thomas shook Tom's head.

The sun remained frozen in space. Thomas's brown face shone bronze. Amazement, realization, and acceptance fell over the ghost within him. "It's just outside the realm of possibilities."

He then looked up at Mary Anne, breathing in her whole valley sheeted in solstice snow before her. On the illuminated Bridge, she felt as if God had given her feet wings to flutter high above a river with more secrets than Styx. Suspending the rock above her head, she swayed, listening to the birds' songs. Seeing the evening star peek through the clouds, she whistled the tune Tom had taught her and the mockingbird and then smiled. "I remember the spirits swimming free around me."

MARY ANNE RANDOLPH THEN SLAMMED the rock toward Jefferson.

AFTER THE EXPERIENCE, MARY ANNE walked around town with a broader, taller, more confident air. Was it because, despite both headlights having been knocked out, she was able to speed her old wood-bodied station wagon to the hospital? Or because she, a skinny bleached white woman, was able to heave a large Negro's body onto her shoulder and haul him down a mountain? Or was it because—at the moment before twilight—she willed herself to break iron chains with calcium-veined limestone?

VIII

The Ghosts

BEAUTIFUL MUSIC. SUCH UNEARTHLY, BEAUTIFUL music flows forth from that woman and has for so many years. Such a voice could only pour from solid stock. I'm proud of her," Elise MacJenkins told Ms. Tzigane as they left Carson Falkland's house one Sunday. "I am proud of Carson's strong, possessed voice that in many ways manifests the spirit of Concord."

What Elise was saying was something we all knew. "And though she doesn't have a great deal of money, she has what others don't: a lineage. A long, unbroken limestone-strong lineage that forms the spine of this town. Laws and religions may fall, but we've always had a Falkland to return to."

THAT NIGHT, CRAZY MARY ANNE Randolph, Carson's faithful pianist, had a frightful dream. Virginia creeper, hissing afire, begged her: "Help me do what Virginia creeper does best, Mary Anne. If you please, help me do what Virginia creeper does best."

* * *

ACROSS TOWN, CARSON FALKLAND, WITH her gray, once-red, hair strewn about her, sat Indian style in her gingerbread house's attic.

She'd been there since before dawn. Unable to sleep on the eve of her deceased younger sister's birthday, she'd risen in the wee hours and crept up the unpainted stairs in her worn white nightshirt. Under the slanted roof and dusty glow, she sifted through stored lives. Existences that, her ancestors had thought, should not be thrown away. So, they'd been packed away in chests—as bones exhumed from crowded European soil—boxed to make room for the expected dead.

Like the Edison lamp burning above, the papers before her were yellow. Old letters, with just names and towns—no addresses needed; a soft-bound black journal, where her great-great-grandfather Zachary had religiously written every day about the weather or whether the mockingbird, whom he named Henry, had sung; a ledger from the old farm: *March 1882, 8 chickens, $9.00, 5 dozen fertile eggs, $1.60.* Now she held the family Bible—hard-bound, too unwieldy to read in bed, but ideal for viewing together in the living room. She carefully opened it up and traced through the names, written in steel-pointed, flourished script. Beside each were dates, hooking life-hoods to births, marriages, and deaths.

There—her seven-times great-grandfather, Cyrus, who'd founded the town—*Death: August 17, 1779.*

Her four-times great-grandfather, Benjamin, who'd joined Andrew Jackson in the War of 1812 and captured fifty British soldiers in the Battle of New Orleans—a victory, even if London and D.C. had already signed a treaty two weeks before. *Death: January 3, 1830.*

Martha, her great-great-grandmother, who built the Church and whose stoic defense of it persuaded the Yankees not to burn it down. *Death: April 2, 1877.*

Josiah, her grandfather, the Mayor who started the Bank and held its funds together during the Depression. *Death: October 9, 1939.*

Most recent, in her own hand (she'd learned to use the steel-tipped pen), were the hooks for her father, Christian; her mother, Sarah; her sister, Anne; her brother-in-law, Daniel; and her latest-living family link, her nephew, John. *Death: August 8, 1958.*

Names and dates, Carson thought. Written as if someone in the future would be around who cared. As if the record-keeping could ascribe some meaning or serve in the future as environmental or cultural history.

But now Carson Falkland, approaching the second bookend of her and her family's life, gravely asked herself, *Who will chronicle my death in this* Bible*? What attic will it rest in once I am gone?*

She thumbed through Cyrus's decayed leather brown journal. *Cyrus of Concord,* she thought. He'd migrated from Pennsylvania to settle the Valley in the 1740s, having received the royal land grant under the stipulation that he'd establish a hundred families in the area.

She read his description of fighting during the French and Indian War.

> It being early in the morning some French were asleep and some eating, but having heard a Noise they immediately betook themselves to their Arms . . . one of the French fired a Gun upon which Col. Washington gave the Word for all us King's Men to shoot. . . .
>
> Some Time after the savage Half King took his Tomahawk

> and Ruthlessly split the Head of the French Captain. . . . He then took out the Captain's brains and washed his Hands with them. . . .

Looking down, she saw an earlier entry.

> And I have spotted where there may be a Town, laying almost 6 miles from the highlands, where a forked shape river has navigable waters. The nearby forests Are Rich and Varied, with massive chestnuts, walnuts, and pines.

And another—

> September 1763, 25 gold coins, militia rewards.

Such a sparse entry compared to the others. *What did he leave out?*

Absentmindedly holding the journal, she left the attic. She urgently dressed in her riding outfit and ran out of her house. The journal dropped from her dresser, onto the floor.

"CARSON," MARY ANNE RANDOLPH, WEARING a giant-brimmed felt hat, whispered without confidence into Leggs's stall, within Betty Joe's barn. Carson was hurriedly rubbing, in large circular motions, a plastic currycomb on the horse's back. "How are you?"

"Mary Anne! How did you know I was here?"

"I just wanted to make sure you were okay."

"I'm sorry, but I'm in a bit of a rush. Yesterday someone at the Museum of the Confederacy called and asked a few questions about Concord's beginnings. They're thinking of moving from Richmond to the old Church here."

"No one knows more about Concord's history than you, Carson."

Carson started picking the horse's feet. "I've got the old family records and stories, but—"

EVERYONE KNOWS THE FALKLAND FAMILY'S story. Old Prof. Rayburn even taught about it in his American history class at Jefferson College. With timelines, illustrations, and an occasional flourish of his hand, Rayburn would lecture how "Cyrus had arrived to the untamed landscape at a time when it looked that the French were going to permanently stake out Appalachia and the western lands. But Cyrus charmed the Indians, displeased with the French for reneging on promises of booty. In exchange for allying instead with the British, he promised the Monocans peace in the highlands and trade with the settlers in town. In honor of the harmony, Cyrus appropriately named, with much pomp and circumstance, the new English settlement Concord.

"The highlands are still unsettled in honor of that promise, though the Indians have long since scattered."

As an added note, Rayburn never failed to mention that he knew the great-great-great-great-great-great-great-granddaughter of Cyrus, and went over to her house every Sunday to hear her sing.

CARSON HEAVED THE SADDLE ONTO the horse. She tightened the girdle. "I'm going up to the caves by Deadman Mountain."

She meant the ones in which Cyrus and the other settlers had lived before starting the town.

"I haven't been up there since father pointed them out to Anne and me when we were little. Anne used to go up there all the time."

"I remember Anne telling me— Why don't you just ask Jethro O'Pitcans to investigate them for you? He's always spelunking."

Placing the bridle over Leggs's ears, Carson shot a look at Mary Anne. Carson viewed Jethro, like Mary Anne, as one of those people who wouldn't know a clue if it smacked him flat on the face. "No. I don't know what I'm looking for. But, I'll know it when I see it."

Crestfallen, Mary Anne started to gaze away, outside the barn, and drift.

Carson reflected on how Mary Anne had become even paler after Anne's death. Carson had never had time to understand Mary Anne, but—

"Mary Anne, would you like to come along?"

"Oh, I don't know. I'm not very good with horses. They don't like me much."

"We'll put you on Molly." Carson pointed across the aisle.

"Carson, I don't see a horse."

"Look closer." Carson grinned.

Mary Anne trod across the aisle, to the stall's grated window. She saw a draft horse lying on her back, legs spread-eagle, airing it out.

"You couldn't spook that animal with a canon." Carson laughed.

Mary Anne heard thunder. The horse, disturbed, rolled onto her belly and stared at crazy Mary Anne. Both blinking, they witnessed each other's third eye. "Are you sure it's a good idea to venture up there today? It feels like rain."

Not a cloud floated in the sky. Carson, who hadn't heard any thunder, went into the tack room, grabbed two headlamps, and looked out the window.

"The weather will hold."

TAKE ME INTO THE WOODS. Take me into the forest as those two women, past middle age but still hearty, rode into the foothills of the Blue Ridge to the bygone settlement of the Falkland family, whose presence in town has remained unbroken. The time: autumn. The second week of October, when the trees change so that when looking into the wood, you are not sure if you're looking out into the environment, or inward, to the memories that haunt the mind.

But, you say, fall is beautiful in many places. But because this is a cross-lands—with the East's orange-podded bittersweet; the Midwest's redbuds; the South's pawpaws, with custardlike mango fruit; and the North's sugar maples, brilliant yellow—Shenandoah's autumn chromatic is the world's finest. Lush, for this is the rainy South, with its summer jungle. Mother Nature must use one of each of her ribbons to wrap the teeming forests for winter.

Over forty-five years had passed since Carson Falkland had ridden this trail: before she moved to New York, before she had started a career as a singer, before her sister had died, and before she returned to Concord to care for her sister's son, John. Her sister, Anne, had died near the caves to which this trail led. And so, after coming back—Carson hadn't come near Deadman Mountain. At this trail's top, at the peaks of the Blue Ridge, in 1716,

Governor Spotswood and his company of explorers, the Knights of the Golden Horseshoe, first viewed the Valley. And Cyrus had trekked the same path down from the mountains to survey the spot that would become Concord. Now, suddenly anxious to unbury the past, Carson restlessly backtracked along Cyrus's steps.

Mary Anne thought about how she knew the trail's past for different reasons. Here, as often happened to her, she'd perceive whispers of Indian spirits. In a blink, she'd catch sight of them carrying a clay coiled pot, hunting, or checking traps. The entities would be there, and then not there—except for small marks, shards still carried by the landscape. Long ago, people traveled the trail because it was well watered. Looking at the springs now, Mary Anne wondered if they were the mountain's tears.

HAVING MADE IT THROUGH THE mixed woods near the Fork River, they came to a small clearing, where several red cedars and pines had grown up. A few stray cows paused briefly from their grazing to watch the women on horses.

Up ahead, Mary Anne had a vision: Sparsely covered copper women? . . . Three sisters? Corn, bean, squash . . . Crying.

From . . . Tears . . . East . . .

. . . arrive

. . . Hawks

. . . screams?

. . . toss my body away?

"ARE YOU SURE YOU HAVE to go ahead up to the caves? Why don't we just stay here and play with the cows?" Mary Anne asked.

"Mary Anne, try to remain focused," Carson said with exasperation.

"Cattle play a big role in the town's history."

"I don't think cows have anything to do with what I'm looking for."

At the other edge of the clearing, they approached some mounds planted with trees. Molly took the unusual step of quickening her pace—causing Mary Anne to fret. "Carson! Help!" Molly stopped as she brought her great black lips around a green apple hanging from a seasoned, scraggly tree.

Mary Anne smiled. Carson stopped as well, and the two friends (*Are we friends?* Carson wondered—*Mary Anne has faithfully taken over playing the piano for me after Anne's death, decades ago*), the companions in music, looked around and realized they were in a forgotten orchard. A few saplings grew around. But one could not mistake the original trees, with layered, broken black bark—like charcoal. Carson dismounted from Leggs and took off his and Molly's bits so they could enjoy the apples.

Yes, these are the same trees, Carson realized. Her eyes felt younger. She saw her sister and herself, as little girls, with their father and mother. Young Carson and Anne had dismounted from their horses and eagerly bit into the first apples they could reach. An expression of confusion had covered Anne's face—framed with bobbed hair—like Mary Anne's. The apple had tasted wooden. Carson's father had laughed and in his manly style (how was it, Carson wondered, that her father, though so well read, had still borne the strength of a frontiersman?) explained that the apples were planted from seed by their grandfather.

"For it was the easiest way to get sugar in these parts," Carson uttered the words spoken by her father.

"That and hard cider," Mary Anne corrected.

"My father didn't mention cider."

"Well, he probably didn't know how to tell a little girl that her grandfather, the Mayor of Concord during Prohibition, was making applejack." Mary Anne spoke, matter of fact.

"How do you know?"

Mary Anne did not say anything.

The revision vexed Carson.

"Nevertheless, even among cider apples, you do find ones that impress the palate." Mary Anne ambled through the orchard and bit into another apple. "Notes of cherry." She smiled.

Sensing tall men and women, Mary Anne stopped. Copper body decorations . . . Mourning . . . Remains in the mounds . . . White men arriving on horses . . . Shooting guns.

Mary Anne jumped onto her horse. She reached out and broke off an apple-laden branch from the tree next to her. She held the bough over Molly's head, carroting the animal downhill.

"Mary Anne!" Carson, with amusement, shouted. "Come on. Why are you leaving?"

Mary Anne held the limb straight up into the air. Molly looked around, wondering how the fruit bough had vanished. "Isn't it enough for the Museum that Elise MacJenkins—who single-handedly reinforced all veterans of the Confederate Army with booze during Prohibition—resides here. Why do we have to conjure up more—?"

"I don't care about the Museum. Suit yourself. I'm going on."

Mary Anne looked at the mound, knowing what remained in it. She examined Carson, who seemed clueless.

Mary Anne then pointed the branch, like a wand, at Carson. Molly turned, following her spell, and they continued along the trail.

* * *

CARSON THOUGHT ABOUT HER SISTER, Anne, and the close friendship she'd had with this odd woman who now rode with her, whom many in town called a loon. As a child, Carson had even teased Anne for playing with the loopy girl. What, besides the piano, had made them friends? "So, what do you have planned for your birthday?" Carson asked.

"How do you know it's going to be my birthday?"

"It is a few days after Anne's, which is today."

"She was three days older—and a lifetime."

"She always told me that playing the piano with you was like falling into a trance, a dream."

"She really said that?"

Carson laughed, nodded—and then frowned. "You know, had Daniel not died also in the accident, I think I would have killed him myself." Carson shuddered with the realization. "Does that make me a horrible person?" Observing the nearby scarlet maple, she thought of her sister's hair, which had been redder than her own. She wondered if it, too, would have been gray now.

"No, Carson. We cannot help what we feel."

They were now in the highlands. The birches, oaks, and maples were at least double trunked. Generations and generations ago, the area must have been logged by the Falklands and perhaps the MacJenkins. Now competing clones had grown up from each stump, supporting leaves that gleamed. Their shapes reminded Mary Anne of arrowheads.

"Carson, it's a beautiful day, but it'll be late before we get back. I want to make a good supper to remember Anne's birthday. If we turn back now, we'll have time to stop again at the apple orchard. I can gather some to make you a pie. Cider apples make good pies."

Carson rolled her eyes. She rode upon a mountain brook and suddenly stopped.

THIS WAS THE MOUNTAIN SPRING'S pool that her sister had named Thumbelina. How could she have stayed away for so long? The water slid down a smooth slide. Deepening the swimming hole were two downstream walls of rocks, forming a V shape. Her family had journeyed here countless times. Here she'd picnicked with Anne, Daniel, and John—a day before she moved to New York. Even though it was colder now than that summer day, Carson wanted to climb off her horse, take off her clothes, and wade into the water. If she did, would Anne be next to her again, as they chatted about—what were they talking about, just the day to day? It was wonderful to have someone with whom Carson could say whatever she wanted and not have to worry about being judged.

"Carson, go get 'em," Anne had said. A very young John was playing with his father in the rapids. "Remember, if you ever need a break, we'll have your room waiting for you at home."

A marble-colored salamander, curiously not yet in hibernation, jumped off a rock and into the water.

Mary Anne envisioned the two walls of rocks as they had been two centuries ago: The stone piles directed all the water through one gated sluice.... Indian braves upstream whipped the water.... Brook trout, caught between rock walls, gate, and whipped water swam frantically about.... Thrashing... Hopeless... Speared... Thrown ashore.

Now, the water sparkled in the clear light. Mary Anne felt

eons back, when the Valley so awed the heavens that the stars each cast a jewel—to shine forever—into the land's waters. Hence the name, clear-eyed daughter of the stars: Shenandoah.

Carson thought of all her lost family. And she thought about how Mary Anne was haunted by her mother, who died giving birth to her.

"Mary Anne, do you still long for your mother?" Carson pushed Leggs ahead.

ALL THE WOMEN IN MARY Anne's family had loose screws. Or, to say it more politely, were of a sensitive mind. It had been this way since 1784, when Molly Moore, Mary Anne's distant foremother, at age eight was captured by a Shawnee Indian and sold into slavery in Canada. Rescued and returned to New Orleans when she was fifteen, she could not escape the nightmares. To help her sleep, an adult-sized cradle was made for her.

"IT'S GETTING DARKER. ARE YOU sure you don't want to go back?"

"Answer the question. How can you miss someone you never knew?" Carson turned and laughed awkwardly.

Mary Anne, hurt, stared back at Carson. She wished she had one those hard apples to throw at her.

They passed under a ruby persimmon tree. Most of its leaves had fallen, but orange bitter fruit still clung to its branches.

"Yes," Mary Anne flatly answered.

"Even though you never knew her?"

"Just as, I suppose, someone who's never had love always longs for it. Or someone who can't have a child—"

Suddenly the color died from the above leaves.

"Carson—"

"Mary Anne, I can't stop now."

MOVING HIGHER, THEY ENTERED A region of the forest where—because of the sudden fluctuations that often occur between storms and drought—conifers, with primitive water-connecting tracheids, beat out their hardwood, veined brothers.

In the woods around her, Mary Anne deciphered shadows of feather-decorated warriors . . . riding to aid red-coated English in a war against French fur traders. . . .

It started to rain. Big drops—the size of white button mushrooms.

"Carson, let's go home."

"I think we're almost there. Look!" Carson aimed Leggs toward a large limestone cliff face. Leggs trotted adroitly through massive flat rocks stacked in Stonehenge-like ways. Molly, bedeviled by the rain, followed in speed. When they reached the outcrop wall covered in crimson Virginia creeper, they dismounted and left their horses under the rock overhang.

"This looks familiar, doesn't it?" Carson's statement was one of hope rather than of certainty. "The cave entrance must be—" She moved along the limestone walls veined by calcium, and brushed over tall goldenrod. Right before her hand fell into the emptiness of the cave covered in vines, Mary Anne stepped in front of her.

"Carson, I do not think you should go in the cave."

"What?"

"I have a feeling—"

"Well, I have a feeling that we'll both get pneumonia if we

don't get out of the rain." Carson pushed Mary Anne aside, sundered the scarlet curtain, and walked into the dark mountain. She lit her carbide lamp.

The cave was vast. Up through the mountain, twisting in many ways, were windows without light. Carson heard the dribble of water around her, though the ground beneath her feet was dry.

Behind her, Mary Anne entered the cavern with her carbide lamp already afire. She scrutinized the walls. "There is another entrance to the cave, Carson."

"How do you know?"

Knowing only that the knowledge had come from the back of her brain, Mary Anne looked at Carson. Against a gust of air, they moved forward, Carson searching for something that could complete the Falkland story—so it could still exist when she was no longer alive to sing and talk and pray and remember. She could hear the horses rustling about outside. On her right, she placed her hand on a greenish inverted-cone formation, which had as a companion a large mineral icicle dripping from the roof above. Mary Anne had disappeared. Carson, figuring she'd gone back to the entrance, did not call out to her, for fear of awakening the stones. Like a maze, several passages departed from each chamber, and she worried about losing her way. She picked up a few pebbles and made an arrow shape out of them on the ground.

In front of her, the walls narrowed. A boulder had fallen from overhead and was wedged in this narrowness, creating a lintel that she fearfully passed under. In the next chamber, her carbide showed the walls moving. Dizzy, she reached out to steady herself. Around her fingers, a spiky mesh jittered and crunched, and then a swarm of cave crickets attacked her, her hair, her shirt. She gathered all her wits to suppress a scream, and she brushed off the infectious sprickets.

She traveled into several other caverns.

In one she saw a deep pit. Her lamp did not show the bottom. From the ground, she nervously picked up a piece of raw copper. The cavern walls were glazed here and there with verdigris metal leaves. She tossed the piece in her hand into the pit. *Click . . . click . . . click . . .* It took ten seconds to stop. Must be three hundred feet, she reasoned with wonder, recalling how her father had taught her to count such distances.

In the next chamber, she saw a blue pool. On the walls above it, minerals had precipitated in rose shapes. Her mother had lovingly painted such a design above the mirror in Carson's bathroom.

She then entered the last chamber, an opening at the westerly side of the mountain. Gray blue crept through the cave mouth, curtained also by vines.

Directly in the middle of the room stood ghost-white Mary Anne Randolph.

"There is nothing here, Carson."

"How do you know?" Carson spoke with spite. She searched carefully, shining her carbide lamp in every crevice. But the cave mouth was large, and though creeper covered it, in a few weeks all the leaves would be gone, letting the elements in. In one area she saw a few Virginia big-eared bats hugging closely to the cave walls, their droppings piled below. But besides them and their dung, this cave—yes, this was the cave of her Falkland ancestors—bore no signs of a past life.

"There must be something!" she gasped. "Oh, I was expecting—I don't know—at least a mark on the wall."

"Carson, before we started this trip, I thought you knew. For you sing so beautifully, oh so beautifully, I thought you sang for the same reason that Anne and I played, to fill the—"

"Where's John? Where's Anne? Where are my parents? Where is some member of my family I can talk to before I die?"

MARY ANNE HEARD, IN THE cave gust, Indian intimations, . . . *hear me singing, I am . . . crying . . . lost . . .*

"Carson, do you know what I see?"

"What?" she snapped.

Mary Anne reached down and picked up a blue lanceolate stone.

Carson seized the spearhead in her hand. "What does it mean?"

"I don't know." Mary Anne sat on the ground. But she did. For it happened in this cave.

PAINTED AND FEATHERED . . . WARRIORS, RIDING

no longer needed . . .

falsely accused of stealing cows . . .

The Falklands' militia . . . took the braves . . .

this cave, made them lie down . . .

. . . twenty-five gold coins.

"CARSON, WHAT DESERVES TO BE remembered?" Mary Anne asked while they consoled each other as dark fell.

Carson thought of the unwritten in Cyrus's journals.

Among so many stories to tell, so many songs to sing, the last of the Falklands heard silence.

IX

The Abandoned Church

THERE WERE NO PROTESTS THE ripe August day we closed Concord's only church for good. Tom Dorian and his team of boys hauled out the pews and the large tiger-striped maple cross, which had been nailed together ever since the Falkland family founded our Virginian town in the 1740s. A Wells boy snatched up the antebellum tabernacle to store his moonshine in. And Jethro O'Pitcans, the town idiot, gleefully made off with the "relic" finger of Saint Christopher in his shirt pocket.

We gave the blue-veined marble baptismal pool to Ms. Tzigane. She quickly converted it to an outdoor bath for her handicapped animals—such as her three-legged dancing black bear, Cassandra. If we needed to baptize, she said we should use the river. We supposed she was right.

Lastly, the great black cherry piano was carefully moved to Ms. Carson Falkland's gingerbread home.

* * *

THIS IS THE STORY OF the church and that lady, Ms. Falkland, who possessed such musical power in her vocal cords, she could have silenced Orpheus in a singing contest. She was not the progeny of a muse or a god, but a chanteuse outside the limits of earthly forces. When she sang in church, with her sister, Anne, playing the piano, we were transported. She had the ability to chant her songs—all at once sending a whisper, a cry, and a wave through the crowd. The notes she sang washed one back to the sea and all the soul's forgotten places. With her songs, she seemed preternatural—like an elegant alien sea angel from the depths of a great peaceful ocean, willing and wanting to take us into her upwelling emotions.

Carson was a bright flame that burned even underwater. She knew, though, as Jethro often proclaimed, that "Concord is a black hole. It sucks you in and never spits you out."

So, she moved to Manhattan and landed a job singing in Saint Patrick's Cathedral, which is right in the city's middle. Her performances received praise, but she was confined to singing religious music. Also, she had a difficult time connecting with the transient church members.

Carson wanted to accomplish more. Within her existed a song about a community, but she didn't know how to release it. The emotions and the story had been brewing in her for as long as she could remember, and she needed to start serving these feelings. How else could she grow stronger?

Yet she did not know what else to do. Her passion to share her love distracted her. On the weekends, instead of staying in and writing music, she ventured out in search of Mr. Right. *What good is all the success in the world without someone to love?* she'd tell herself as she slinked out of her room to go to parties, dances, and bars.

She had extended her soul to a few men. One night at a bar, she stumbled upon a young doctor. His face was so flat, long, and freckled, he thought himself ugly. But she saw a gentleness in his half-moon–shaped eyes that made her trust him. With his raspy, playful voice, he compelled her to smile. His embraces were strong and graceful, and she swore she felt energy moving between their hearts. She wanted him to hold her more in his mighty, weathered arms.

THERE WERE OTHERS: A CUTE blond boy with a chiseled face, who pounced and showered her with kisses. He skipped as he walked, and though he was poor and working hard, he was always ready to buy her a drink and laugh. "One more go," he once proclaimed as they were stepping through a revolving door. He grabbed her close around the shoulder, and they twirled around in laughter an extra time.

IN THE END, THE MEN chose not to choose her. However, she'd enjoyed the dates—even if they'd involved going around in circles.

LOVE. SNOW. THE CITY. CARSON hated and loved the snow in New York because it was beautiful. When it snowed, she wished she were in love, proud of herself, and able to share her love proudly. Sometimes, particularly during her fourth year in New York, she'd stand on the top step at Saint Patrick's and watch the small white hexagons falling. Eyes focusing out, welcoming all the flakes into her vision, she'd bring into her mind the cars and people slowly trekking through the white haze of Fifth Avenue. Then, before she'd leave, she'd look down at her black wool jacket and stare at the individual crystals melting away.

It was during this season that Carson's sister, Anne, and her husband died in an accident, winter climbing near Deadman Mountain. Cold with grief, Carson packed up her suitcases and moved back to her father's gingerbread home to care for Anne's son, John. She sang to us during her sister's funeral, this time with Mary Anne Randolph playing the piano, and again she sluiced us into her world. The tears in her voice floated over the pews; if we'd been brave enough, we could have reached out and grasped the salty sound in our hands. Carson had returned. Though her chords quivered with sorrow, the sound still rose with uncanny fire and life.

She took up teaching choir at the local colleges. She woke up early every morning to fix breakfast and pack lunch for John. She drove him to school so he was punctual, and she was always one of the first parents in the row when it was time to pick him up. When John was in high school, she even traveled to his away-from-home football games. One could hear her voice—the beaming, sonorous voice of Carson Falkland—crying from the stands, "Go get them, John!" or, "That's my sister's boy out there!"

Father Biblers came over every Sunday for dinner, after which he'd tutor John in French in the upstairs study. As Ms. Falkland would clean up the dishes, she'd often think about her life in New York. She'd reminisce about the parties and the performances she'd been a part of, and the evenings she'd hoped for. She imagined the love that might still be in the world for her. Then she'd picture John, sometimes strongly and gamesomely playing about the house, other times quietly receding from everyone—as if his sea blue eyes hid the deep's saddest secrets. She worried about him. Putting away the plates, looking about the empty kitchen, feeling the quiet night seep into her home, she'd thank God for the great and scary gift of having a child.

The evening John scored the winning touchdown in the Shenandoah Regional Championships, his teammates ran into the end zone, where he was on his knees, praising the Lord. They threw him onto their shoulders and paraded around the field. Ms. Falkland cried as this was happening and reflected how at one time she, too, had held promise. People had perceived her as they now saw John—young and full of illustrious potential. And she had promised to herself that she'd share her songs with the Earth. She did not want God thinking He'd wasted a gift on her. *Am I the dumb servant who buried his master's gold?* she wondered. Sometimes, she loathed everyone in town and their seemingly provincial visions. But she loved John and Concord that night. He had carefully caught her promise, flying haphazardly through the dark, and gracefully carried it into the scoring zone. The evening was cold. The bleachers she stood in were rickety. Power was in the air as the crowd, wrapped in frayed knits, sang the Fighting Blue's song, held hands, and swayed side to side.

"YOU KNOW, CARSON, I'M STILL not over Anne's death," Mary Anne Randolph confessed while standing beside her. The spectators continued cheering for John and his team. Everyone in town thought Mary Anne was crazy because she claimed to hear voices in her head. But Carson's sister had been her best friend; Matilda Philips had taught them both piano. When Anne and Mary Anne played pieces together, one could see Mary Anne's nervous mind settling down.

"I can no longer talk to her." Mary Anne's red eyes filled with tears. "She was the only woman I could really talk to."

Carson thought about how Mary Anne's own mother, Blanche LeBlanc, died giving birth to her. She also remembered that Mary Anne had a miscarriage the year after Anne died.

"Your sister had such a strong, motherly instinct." Mary Anne's bobbed white hair shook like a solid helmet around her sobbing face. "You do, too. But it's hard for me to talk to anyone, even you, Carson. I missed so much talking with Anne. I miss it—every day of my life."

And Ms. Falkland—crying, too—put her arms around Mary Anne Randolph, the craziest woman in Concord.

CARSON DECIDED TO HAVE A little going-away party for John right before he was to start at the University of Virginia. Before dinner one night, she had sent him and Father Biblers upstairs and told them not to think about coming down until eight. She then checked on her Crock-Pot simmering with lamb in an apricot and brown sugar sauce and quickly set up the surprise dinner party. Because she felt the priest a terrible actor, unable to tell even a white lie, she had kept him in the dark about the matter.

By the time she was taking out the lamb at seven thirty, the guests had arrived. She'd invited his football teammates, a few of his old teachers, and John's other close friends. They decided to creep upstairs and surprise John while he had his nose in the books. One at a time, they slowly slid up the staircase. Then Ms. Falkland, smiling broadly, swung open the study doors.

Mrs. MacJenkins covered her mouth; she couldn't believe the priest was only wearing, of all things, his collar.

John looked up at us, his sea blue eyes saying *I'm sorry, I didn't know how to stop him, and, oh God, I most feared your finding out.* His blond bangs fell in front of his face, and he pushed them out of the way and stared up at us again. He raised himself, and his whole being shuddered, as if his soul were being forced outside his body. Embarrassment, guilt, and anger crashed through him. His football buddies stared at him, confused how this could be the same wide receiver who was nearly impossible to tackle. John grabbed the pewter letter opener with the football handle from the desk and turned around. Grinning, he thrust it into the priest's left eye, who—screaming like a haggardly hog—ripped it out, ran, and then leaped through the study's window, shattering it. John then turned the opener toward himself, shrugging. Meeting his eyes with her own, Ms. Falkland screamed his name. He dug the dagger into his heart. She reached him as he brought it completely through his chest, and she cradled him as his blood gushed from his breast and all over her middle-aged body.

"GOD HAS A PLAN," THE new priest announced the following Sunday. Father Biblers amazingly survived and had been transferred to some unknown location. The new rector refused to allow anyone who'd taken his own life to be interred into our cemetery, so Carson buried John in her backyard, next to the plots she promised to black-as-ink Tom Dorian and his white wife, Dahlia.

"We all need to learn to accept His plan. I know these times do not make sense, but we must keep our faith in this Church and God," the new priest warned. But as he expelled these words, Ms.

Falkland, wearing a black linen dress, rose from her pew at the front and started to walk out. Shaking her head in grief as she stepped down the aisle, she swore she'd never return.

Names, Carson thought. *Names in an empty crowd.* She remembered how in Manhattan she would escape into the mass of people, where she had hoped to find a way to share her voice and someone whose heart connected with her own. She wanted to have a great, linked life. All was lost. Her story would never be told. Its senselessness, though, would never escape her.

"What do you mean, 'God has a plan'?" Mary Anne Randolph shouted, standing up from her place at the piano and halting the priest's homily. Mrs. MacJenkins ripped off her hat so that she and those around her could have a better view. Now at the door of the church, Carson turned and looked up the aisle. The stained-glass windows, white pews, and walls glowed with a golden-orange light from Mary Anne.

"You heard me! What do you mean, 'God has a plan'?" Her voice was high and creaky, both angelic and demonic. Fear froze the priest. "You heard me. What do you mean?"

She strutted from her stool at the piano. Pointing her finger, she went right toward the Father. She glared at him with an angry, fiery look of an oriental dragon. Her body held that serpent, ready-to-strike tension to it. Her dress was the color of copper. Shaking with divine rage, she leapt onto the altar.

"Look at me!" she called to the priest and then to us, her white hair rising from her head and floating about, like electricity in a lightning globe. "Look there," she ordered, pointing to Ms. Falkland. She cried aloud as she shook her hands above her head. Flinging her arms out as if she were being nailed onto a cross, she screamed, "Oh, the pain. Our slavery! My friend Anne! My momma, Blanche! Why?" Weak and dangling, she raised her head to heaven and uttered, *"Eloi, Eloi, lama sabachthani?"*

Then she fainted, falling from the mystic, invisible cross she'd been nailed to and collapsing onto the altar. The resounding noise she made upon hitting the table sent ripples over the pews and up to the balcony where the colored folk sat.

NAMES, CARSON THOUGHT. *NAMES IN an empty crowd. So many stories to tell. So many songs to sing. So many lives to live and connect with. So much never accomplished. Where does God fit into all this? Will there be love? What is success? Where does hope lie in a town where one cannot escape the past?* Eloi, Eloi, lama sabachthani. *My God, my God, why have you abandoned me? No. How could I be so foolish? How could I fail so much?*

THE FOLLOWING SUNDAY, CARSON FALKLAND opened her front door to find the entire congregation standing on her porch and in her yard. Mary Anne Randolph smiled broadly as Ms. Tzigane held her hand. Then Mrs. MacJenkins, who hadn't missed a day of Mass ever since her grandson went off and returned from Korea, stepped forward and with teary eyes proclaimed, "We decided— We decided that we would not return to church either. We would return to you."

On her gingerbread porch, Carson Falkland leaned her head against the doorway and cried. Covering her ocean blue eyes with her hand as her soft red hair came loose from its bun, she tried to pull herself together. Then she just let herself weep. "Won't you come in—," she requested through her tears. "Won't you all come into my home?"

* * *

AND IF YOU STROLL BY that gingerbread house on Sunday, we hope you still will be able to hear all of us singing—singing with Carson Falkland as she sends her sonorous, primordial voice through her father's gingerbread house, into our hearts, and through this town's psyche. Word of this great chanteuse spread throughout the Valley, and pilgrims flock to her home. She welcomes them all. Crazy Mary Anne Randolph plays the cherry piano. And as Carson lets herself go, we try to learn her ancient, mystic sea-filled tone as we link our spirits and mourn with one another over how lonely and purposeless life can be. Forming a huddle and wrapping our arms around Carson, we remember John, Anne, and all the old souls torn too fast from our grasp. We picture all the strangers in the crowd whose names we will never know, the playful voices that do not love us, the revolving doors that stopped, and the blades that cut too short the candles of the bright. We tell Ms. Falkland that even though God may be cruel, we will always believe in her song. Nobody, not even Jesus, is ever going to take away that love and faith from us.

X

The Strangers

HER BREASTS WERE THIN, LONG, and deflated. Under her robe they shifted back and forth as she pedaled in the back of the baby blue tandem bicycle. She liked that she was free to look around. Especially here, on the cliffside road, high above the Fork River in the Concord Pass, past Mrs. MacJenkins's cabin. The river below flowed through a canyon of navy blue limestone.

With her satchel on her back, she sighed peacefully. The bird-shaped shadows that broke through the trees swooped across her and her companion—shading them black, white, orange, green.

Her companion, Mr. Silversmith, noticed that the wind gusted so wonderfully because the pass created a tunnel effect. With deliberation, he pedaled, her feet moving with his time.

They stopped at a high place on the road, at a little shoulder, stories above the water. She hopped off the bike first. "Wine-berries," she announced, pointing out a few dozen red fruits. He followed her, and together they snacked on the tangy berries hanging from the hairy, thorny stems.

"Leave some for birds," Ms. Tzigane ordered. A daddy longlegs crawled over a leaf next to her hand. She opened her palm, letting it climb across it to reach the next branch.

Careful not to trip, they held each other's hands as they stepped down the scores of centuries-old stone steps along the cliff face. They made it to the riverbank.

Out of her satchel she took Lucky, a painted turtle whose naturally fire-red-and-green shell had been fractured on the left side by Tom Dorian's truck years ago. With the help of Ashley Reeves, the vet; some wire; and fiberglass plates—Ms. Tzigane had nursed the animal back to health. Today, it was time to let Lucky go. She put the reptile down on the rocks. Lucky—still a little dizzy from the bike ride—poked her yellow-and-red-striped head out of her shell.

Ms. Tzigane took off her robe. She sat down on the jagged indigo stones. She placed her leathery feet into the river, just cold enough to awaken her spirit. Slipping her thighs in, she then pushed forward. Not wanting to leave her mistress's side, Lucky fearlessly plunged off the rock and plopped into the water.

Mr. Silversmith followed, and the couple, in midlife, floated in the current of that full deep-blue water just after the hellish rapids that inner-tubers affectionately call Devil's Kitchen. Across from the cliff, the calm water meandered around a sandy bend.

As they drifted, laughing, Lucky swam by them and then, reluctantly, away. Ms. Tzigane waved good-bye. Silversmith smiled and wondered how—of all the places in the world—he ended up in the Fork River.

HE'D ARRIVED IN CONCORD IN the winter of 1952. His well-polished black Chevrolet two-door sedan stalled out right in front of Ms. Tzigane's wooden inn, located down by the river road. The long plank-wood white house, with up- and downstairs wraparound verandas, had been built as a resting place for horse-and-buggy or river travelers.

Upon hearing that Mr. Silversmith was a jeweler, Ms. Tzigane's first speculations were on how she might lift a few rings off him. But as she was serving him sleep-inducing tea and he reached to take his cup, she noticed the black numbers on his left forearm: 179217.

She spilled the tea, some dribbling onto her robes, bracelets, and bare feet. As he tried to help her clean it up, she apologized and then asked him if her people were given similar tattoos.

"The Zigeunerin were in a different camp at Auschwitz," he said, unsure.

"HOW DID I END UP here?" Silversmith laughed aloud as he submerged himself in the water. He opened his eyes. Speckled with clay, the liquid looked gold-flaked. Diving deeper, he sensed the cold groundwater seeping up from the river bottom. He settled himself on the colder layer, held his nose, flipped over, and looked up at the wobbling, rippling nova high above his head. With her long white skirt still on, the Blue Gypsy eclipsed the sun for a moment before she plunged down.

She reached and gently rubbed the back of his neck as he wrapped his arms around her.

Moments later, as they swam upstream, he suggested they wade along the riverside.

"But rocks are slippery," she stated.

"It is better to stumble than to too tired become," he replied.

* * *

NOW LYING ON A ROCK, they let the warm rays douse their bodies—each lotioned by the other.

Silversmith looked at the wild woman resting beside him. He couldn't believe that this strange lady had become so intertwined in the small Southern town of Concord. And he still felt like a stranger. "How did you with Elise friends become?"

"Why you ask?"

"You do not seem just like someone with whom she would normally friendly be."

"Why say that?" Ms. Tzigane rolled over onto her side and looked at him. Behind her, her robes waved in the breeze. Silversmith stared at Ms. Tzigane's naked body. She got the hint.

"One day," she explained to him, "Simon Donald convinced Elise to have me over for bridge game with club. Elise was not pleased when she discovered I did not know how to play game. But while Carson Falkland was showing me practice hand, I warned that cards announced arrival of a hostile presence. Then William Carlisle sent golf ball crashing through Elise's living room window."

"How did you predict?"

She grinned. "Elise saw that I could read cards one way or another. She quickly enlisted me as bridge partner. However, it was months before she'd put out her good silver in my presence. But now, we haven't lost game in years."

"Why have you not gone to larger tournaments?"

"Elise MacJenkins? She don't like big cities. Says there too many foreigners."

"Will you read my cards sometime?"

"Roma only tell fortunes to strangers." She peered upstream. Two entities tubed through Devil's Kitchen. She rose, took her and Mr. Silversmith's clothes off the sycamore sapling, and put on her robe.

Mary Francis and Lee Anne, George MacJenkins's twin teenage daughters, bounced down the rapids. They both have streaks of Indian, inherited from their mother, Nancy, and grandmother, Flying Bird—a Monocan who'd escaped her Indian reservation as a young savage and camped her whole adult life in our pass. "Give my regards to your father and vultures!" Ms. Tzigane shouted and waved.

"We will!" they responded in sync. A breath of wind rustled the branches of the giant sycamores and pines, sending a few leaves and needles into the air.

"You're not stranger in town," Ms. Tzigane stated.

Mr. Silversmith shrugged his eyebrows.

THE DAY AFTER MS. TZIGANE spilled tea on Mr. Silversmith, she informed him that Concord's jeweler, Mrs. Rubie Wellington, had recently died. We were in desperate need of a new one. None of us knows a possum's behind about setting a stone or fixing a watch.

Upon seeing the space along with Ms. Tzigane's hopeful face, he decided to set up shop. He ripped down the gaudy yellow-and-black Victorian curtains. On the counters, he placed large mirrors and prisms, which in daylight set the gems on fire.

It was great to have Mr. Silversmith in town because, as Matilda Philips said, he is a German—and so he was really good at fixing watches. At the same time, we didn't have to feel guilty about buying from someone from that Nazi-loving country, because he's a Hebrew and his people had been gassed. As long as a bunch of his tribespeople didn't come down here to Concord and attempt to take it over—as the Mormons did in Bassville—we were right pleased to have an Israelite around to show that we had no prejudice whatsoever. It's not like we had to share a pool with him.

Sure, he'd sometimes hear whispering behind his back. (Parents wanted to point out to their kids what a Jew looked like. And a few folks had fears that he might be—like those Jews in Hollywood—a Communist.) But beside those small insignificant happenings, we went out of our way to make him feel at home.

MARY ANNE RANDOLPH BROUGHT HIM a beautiful honey-and-cherry-glazed ham and said if he was ever hungry to come over for supper. He still looked too thin.

GEORGE MACJENKINS ASKED HIM IF he wanted to go deer hunting sometime.

Mr. Silversmith then told George that he would eat only kosher meat.

"Like pickles? I always see that, kosher dills. Thought it meant they were both salty and sweet. . . ."

Silversmith explained further. He'd hunt only if he were starving.

"But without practice, how would you know how to kill anything?"

WHEN CARSON FALKLAND INVITED HIM to her annual Christmas party, Mr. Silversmith always kindly sent his regrets. He did this repeatedly, even though Ms. Falkland explained to him that it was just a cocktail shindig where she and the rest of Concord's upper crust ate fine shrimp brought in from the Chesapeake, got drunk off eggnog, and stood around the piano singing Christmas carols. Why wouldn't he want to come?

Finally, one December, more than a decade after arriving in Concord, he sent Ms. Falkland her RSVP envelope back with the "plan on seeing you there" box checked. And when he arrived, his arm was nestled behind Ms. Tzigane's back. She wore a brand-new dress of red, forest green, and gold. He wore a black suit with a forest green tie. His full, curly hair fell quite princely, quite angelically, behind his ears.

Even at a boring party, those two would have had a great time. But this party was not boring. With Mary Anne Randolph, they talked about the ghosts of Concord, and with Rachel Stetson they spoke about her travels as a reporter. Ms. Tzigane would grab Silversmith by the hand and give a playful glance. They'd fetch each other drinks. And when Mary Anne Randolph began to play the piano, they ventured onto the living room dance floor. Proving her charms were resistant to age, Ms. Tzigane kicked her legs over her head, threw a cartwheel, and dipped her back. And Mr. Silversmith, instinctively, knew how to support her.

Toward the end of the night as the evening quieted down, we gathered around, and Ms. Tzigane told us one of her Gypsy tales.

"On eve of first Christmas after our Lord died," she said, "Gypsies built church of stone and Gaje—that's you people—built one of cheese. They agreed to exchange buildings, with you Gaje also giving Gypsies five pennies. But you Gaje had no money, so you owed Gypsies.

"Well, Gypsies had big party and ate all that cheese. But you Gaje never gave Gypsies five pennies. So, Gypsies are still begging for their due payment. And, since we ate our own Church, instead of worshiping, we feast!"

* * *

BY THE WATER'S EDGE, SHE looked at him with her deep-gray, timorous eyes. "Why you raise your eyebrows?" Ms. Tzigane asked. "Come." He stood up, on the edge of the rock, with her. She affectionately wrapped her arms around his waist and then leaned forward—pushing him into the water with her.

The late-afternoon light seemed especially bright as they made their way up past the deep pool to a series of small terraced waterfalls. After besting the current of the first terrace, they made it to a place between the second and third. Ms. Tzigane held Mr. Silversmith's hand as they settled in the natural Jacuzzi below the third terrace. Then, with a curiosity of what would happen, Ms. Tzigane leaned her head back, against the stone shelf.

The water streamed over her head, creating a liquid shell. The sudden experience of having the water stream so perfectly made her laugh ecstatically. Mr. Silversmith did, too, in part because she was laughing so hard.

She grabbed Mr. Silversmith by the hand and pulled him back. Inside a double bubble, they laughed together with their echoes and then turned to each other and kissed—letting the shell cave in on them.

They swam back to the large indigo rocks. After pulling their books out of their satchels, they laid down their towels in a boulder's water-worn hollows.

It had taken some time for Ms. Tzigane to learn how to read English. Elise had taught her in an effort to make her more "civilized." For even with Elise's support, people thought the Gypsy was feral. Ms. Tzigane had claimed that it was hard to trust the written word, for "it has no eyes, no tongue, no face." But, like a blind woman given sight, she soon fell in love with the unlimited supply of stories. Mr. Silversmith shared that love—albeit for more scholarly reasons—and at night, after they'd eaten (for both hated eating alone), he'd read her Thomas Mann and Stephen Crane, and she'd read him Emily Dickinson or Sherwood Anderson. The evening would grow late, and both being tired, they'd fall asleep in the same davenport. Slowly, the space between them grew smaller and an embrace appeared in sleep.

STRETCHING OUT AS MUCH AS possible on the rocks, Silversmith looked at his trim, scarred body and thought about how strange it was that anyone, especially the weathered, striking woman next to him, would be attracted to it. It had once been a skeleton—with skin sliced, yellow, covered with sores, bruised, and lice-ridden. A tree with its branches cut off. At the end of words.

A heron swooped low, and Ms. Tzigane, with her round face, predicted rain by evening. Silversmith chuckled and reached inside his satchel, pulled out a little box, and then sat next to the Blue Gypsy. She was reading Eudora Welty's "The Wide Net."

"Keja?" he asked, calling her by her real name, which no one in town knew except him. Tzigane was a last name she'd hurriedly made up when she landed in America.

"One second. Two pages left."

He smiled, sat down next to her, and placed his feet in the water. Two small rainbow perch nibbled on his long toes. The sun neared the mountaintops. Its silver reflectance ran over the water like a blanket, right to them.

"Wonderful story. What is it?"

He turned around and showed her the fiery blue-diamond ring.

She cried with joy in his arms. Then he pulled away and

asked, "I was wondering.... I was hoping that we could have a Rabbi marry us."

They rode back in silence. And that night, they thought back to their first lives. Each alone, they both spoke out loud what they had always wanted to say to each other but had never had the strength, time, or finesse to.

"I managed to make it back to Berlin soon after the War," Mr. Silversmith spoke as he ate an omelet. "But in the rubble I knew no one. The Synagogue where my father had . . . even the ghosts . . . no more."

"All my caravan. Gone," Ms. Tzigane said as she ate stewed nettles browned in pig fat. "All shot one early fall morning outside Belgrade."

"Ilse and I had a daughter, Renate, whom we sent off to England in July of 1939. We . . . threw her onto the train.

After I managed to make it to England, I became very aware that I was wearing all I owned—just some charity clothes. . . . Renate did not recognize me when I saw her, in a blue skirt and white blouse. She had a full proper family there. . . . I let her—I just had to let her stay."

"I dug myself out of pit at dark. From Belgrade I wandered by night—stealing chickens, apples, potatoes, and pigs; foraging on wild plants. For one year, my only companions were animals. Finally, I broke into Greece."

"What saved me was faith. Every day I told myself that Providence—I cannot believe I still speak of it—that Providence was watching me. Nothing happens just by chance."

"What saved me was being Gypsy. Had I not spent my whole life wandering back and forth over Europe and Asia, learning how to steal, silence dogs, ride wild horses, live in outside? Do not fight back. Stay always on surface. Move fast."

"'There must be some constancy in life,' my father, with his strong, rough voice, told us at dinner—the night after Kristallnacht our Synagogue wrecked. '. . . Prevents igniting into madness.' My stone foundation . . . transcends time and this Earth."

"There is tale that Jews and Gypsies are enemies because Gypsy King Pharaoh asked Moses to make Nile waters flow back, something he could not. When Pharaoh's engineers did so, he mocked Moses's God, who cursed Gypsies to wander forever. But we love wandering."

"And Torah says, 'After the doings of the land of Egypt shall ye not do . . . and in their ordinances shall ye not walk,' and Gypsy means Egyptian, no?"

One evening, early in their romance, he'd gone over for dinner and seen her stick a skewer into a dead hedgehog's hind leg.

Skillfully, she loosened the skin from the bone. Then, putting the hole in the leg to her mouth, she puffed up the porcupine until it looked like a spiky blowfish. Tying off the hind leg's air hole, she shaved off the quills and then stuffed the rat-looking carcass with black pepper, garlic, and butter. When she finished roasting it, she enthusiastically set it on the table.

"I cannot eat this," he'd said. "Not only does it not have hooves or chew its cud, but I do not know how it was slaughtered."

"It was dead when I found it. Don't worry. I know how it died. My bobcat Bobby killed it and brought it to me in bed this morning. I tell her no, but she was so proud."

"What divides is evil. To live is to have dialogue. Death is drying up, flowing backwards. Rules of life? Rules are to celebrate and not save, and to break Gaje's rules and win!"

"I will not allow the Nazis any more victories. Whom I marry is . . . It is only through praying that I can protest."

"I'M SORRY," SHE EXPRESSED A few days after his proposal. "But one behind cannot sit on two horses. And I like my old nag. There must be another way."

When he told her there wasn't, that if he could not marry her, he needed to stop seeing her, she was humiliated.

"You can't expect me to live life like an animal," he argued.

"You're worse than German," she shot back.

Within a week, Elise MacJenkins, upset that the Jew had shaken her bridge partner, causing them to lose a rubber, stormed into his shop and threatened to send a flaming bottle of moonshine through his store window unless he rekindled his romance with the Blue Gypsy.

HE LEFT CONCORD ON A Sunday. We saw his well-polished black Chevrolet two-door sedan leave, his glimmering stones packed in the backseat. His automobile did not stop, not even backfire, as it passed Ms. Tzigane's house—although she perched in her sunroom's bay window all day.

A FEW DAYS LATER, SIMON Donald stopped by to check on the Blue Gypsy. A big tropical storm had come up from the Gulf of Mexico and was drenching Appalachia. Ms. Tzigane stowed away in her inn with her handicapped animals. The river outside swelled from the rainfall surging down from the mountains and pass. Simon sat with her in silence, petting her paraplegic dachshund, Clea. Then, when the floodwaters reached her front porch steps, from her lap she set down Paprika, her pawless red fox, and marched onto her veranda. There, she began to howl into the wind like a wolf, softly but strongly—not calling, but giving the unloved spirits names:

Putzina
Nanosh
Zurka

Kore
Hanzi
Mala
Jan
Yojo
Rupa
Pulika
Lyuba
Liza . . .

She bayed for almost a half hour. When she finished, the rain abated. Exhausted and drenched, she went back into her living room. With Simon watching her, she spoke by the fire.

"We had just passed outskirts of Belgrade when Germans surrounded our caravan. Our dogs did not listen to us as they attacked Germans, who quickly shot them. They hauled away our horses and ransacked our belongings—even ripping off our earrings, necklaces, and bracelets. For some reason, they missed the gold chain sewn on my son's shirt.

"They then forced us on some trucks, already stuffed with horrified Jews. We didn't know them, and they didn't know us. Strange to be together.

"Germans dumped us out of trucks. Ash and burnt stumps littered ground. Fog we breathed was mixture of smoke and mist. Through haze, I could see bog and river. I thought, 'If only I can get to . . .' But three stiff machine gunners and twelve rifled men stood by. I hoped, if I died, I would haunt them, drag them back to this horrible place!

"They ordered us to dig trench. Jews, fearfully silent, were made to kneel before it. Gunners fired.

"Nazi toads turned to us, and we begged and wailed. My mother flung curses. My father and husband lunged toward Germans, who shot. With my son, Zurka, I jumped forward, into pit. As bodies fell on top us, I wrapped Zurka and me and our faces in my robe. We were in little cocoon. As bodies continued to fall onto us, we—how do you say it?—acted possum.

"The gunners had hit Zurka on shoulder—wound not too bad. But Nazis were firing more rounds into grave. They started shoveling cold sand into us. I covered Zurka's mouth to quiet his tears, to keep him silent. But he began to panic, crying in his honey voice, and bleeding—so much blood. He could not make it to night, when I would dig myself out. Scared, he was in such pain. So when fear overtook him, I hugged him close, covering his small nose and mouth with my hand and—"

The muscles in her shoulders, arms, and face fell spiritless.

"Water does not look back. I regret jumping forward, yes. But water does not look back."

Ms. Tzigane opened a pine chest in her living room and took out a white wool shirt with a small gold chain sewn to it and a bloodstain on the shoulder. She held it against her breasts, breathing it in.

She threw the shirt into the lit fireplace. Numb, she watched the flames incinerate the last remains.

HEADING SOUTH ON ROUTE 11, Mr. Silversmith slammed on his brakes. In the diminishing rain, he got out of his Chevrolet and knelt before the animal he'd almost run over. He picked her up.

A painted turtle. Silversmith could see the healed fractures on the shell's left side.

* * *

SIMON LEFT. WITH HER HARP, like a mystic sail, between her legs, Ms. Tzigane played an old melody as she stared at the red glowing embers. Her storm-door began knocking in the wind. She broke herself from her daze and listlessly opened up her front door to stop the rapping.

"I was wondering. I was wondering if you'd like to share with me some apples and honey. You can have a hedgehog if you would like. Also, I found Lucky trying to cross the highway. I think we should keep her here. She seems to not know to stay away from the road."

She grabbed him by his tie, pulled him close, and they made love right there, in her doorway, with Lucky, the painted turtle; Carolina, the earless rabbit; and Rupa, the beakless woodpecker watching.

IN SUMMER, THEY STILL RIDE that tandem bicycle to the river. Now, though, sometimes she leads. When she pedals, she often speeds, howling in ecstasy. With a mixture of joy and fright, he screams, too. He figures after all he's been through, if he flies off a cliff on a baby blue bicycle with someone he loves and crashes into the mountain waters of the Fork River—he might as well enjoy the thrill. There are worse ways to go.

Three or four nights a week, come summer or winter, she carries out in the yard his gold-and-silk German eiderdown for them both to sleep on.

"Don't do that," she requests.

"What?"

"Point out shooting stars."

"Why again?"

"They're souls. Sometimes they need to be able to run away and not be pointed out."

"I LOVE WIND!" MS. TZIGANE gasps, the air flowing over them while they fall asleep. "Makes my dreams feel so free!"

This woman, he thinks. *This Gypsy is crazy. Absolutely wild. Like an animal. Tactless.*

This man, she thinks. *This Jew is so stale. So rigid, stiff, like board. So worried about making mistake that he—*

Her whiskerless bobcat wanders by. Cassandra, the three-legged dancing bear, tied to a close tree, snores.

And I love her.

And I love him.

How fortunate, they both feel, to have met each other in the autumn of their lives, as strangers in a strange land—where they're free to experience such a spring love.

XI

The Ancients

THE STORIES OF A RIVER and a person do not usually weave together. A river and the wedge it cuts are so very ancient that it should lie outside the timescale of a human's life, even one so protracted as that of Elise MacJenkins. For a human, time means a progression from conception to birth to maturity to cricketness to dust. A waterway, on the other hand, may meander as it grows older, but it does not weaken if the climate stays.

The Concord Pass was beautiful in its age. The water fell through the mountains, exposing layers of buried matter to the windy pathway. At some places along the Fork River, one could find gigantic purple boulders, jagged and sheeted, yet smooth and baked in the Confederate sun. At other sites, one could lie on large, rough granite stones—ingrained with white and clear specks. As the boulders glittered in the hot light, we spread out on them.

The river had changed slowly over the decades, noticeably only when great floods had brought stones down from the mountains. Growing in the surfaces of the rough rocks were lichens—light green, sometimes greenish-orange, colonies growing imperceptibly from year to year. One wondered how ancient, then, was the colony that covered the great, house-sized boulder we called Pumpkin Rock.

OLD LADY MACJENKINS WAS THE most ancient person in town—and had been for as long as anyone could remember. Her face was so wrinkled, when she closed her eyes she looked like a crinkled map of Concord County. We believed she was older than Methuselah, the 150-foot-tall black walnut tree that stood, gnarled and grand, in her cabin's front yard. When asked about her years, she said she had stopped counting after she reached one hundred. We figured we better do the same.

The only person in town who came close to her age was Alistair MacGregor. The septuagenarians and octogenarians averred that before Alistair arrived to Concord, the soil was exhausted from the tobacco plantations. Having lived part of his life with the Monocan Indians, Alistair composted the organic waste from town; grew mixed fields of corn, beans, and squash; and danced naked to the plant, rain, and sun gods.

As the germinator of life, he stood every bit of six feet two inches and had thick bones rumored to be made of diluvian limestone. Over his great skeleton stretched skin—scaled like persimmon bark. He intimidated even Death. Perhaps they were brothers. Watching Alistair reap his fields with his black walnut–handled scythe, one could see why the Dark Angel feared paying his sibling a visit.

Old Lady MacJenkins had money, though no one knew exactly how much. She claimed she'd inherited her assets from a prestigious European relative. But everyone knew she had acquired a bundle bootlegging throughout the Valley during Prohibition. She'd invested in precious metals and gems, which she stored in several safes throughout her house. The rest she used to maintain two large plots of property and one hell of a sophisticated still.

A few people over the years tried to place their hands on her dough. Most hit one of the trip wires, tied to bells, which ran around her house. However, one man—Dick Bush—did successfully enter her home one evening while she was sleeping. He'd done some bushwhacking for her a few weeks before, yet she didn't invite him back, because he'd failed to successfully remove a pesky juniper that had taken root underneath her mailbox. He had, however, somewhat acclimated her dogs to his smell, as he had taken his lunch hour to roll around with them.

Not able to find her gold in the main part of the house, he figured that she stored it in her bedroom. He snuck up her great walnut staircase, down the long hall lined with green oriental rugs, and into her gold-cross-bedecked sleeping chamber. An ornate Austrian cross, which was also a clock, hung over her mantel. Sapphire and emerald rosaries draped every lamp, doorknob, and hooked structure in the room.

Screw the gold, the robber thought. He opened his knapsack and began to fill it with her religious memorabilia.

NOW, OLD LADY MACJENKINS ALSO collected dogs. There were always at least five or six of them around the house. At this point in her story, Frederick was alive, an English mastiff–Great Dane mix, about the size of a pony. She also had Captain, who looked like an oversized German shepherd with a leopard coat. There was Onyx, given to her by Simon Donald. He claimed the dog was a Newfoundland, but everyone knew Simon had slipped some black bear into the dog's genome. She had the deaf, albino Irish wolfhound, Whitey. Lastly, was her coddled Walter, a blood–basset hound mix.

All of these rascals slept in their lady's bedroom—fans blowing and them snoring—it was like a postmodern percussion band up there. You could hear the racket as you walked by Mrs. MacJenkins's house after dark. We surmised she was the loudest snorer of them all.

Anyway, most of her dogs snuggled together on a queen-sized feather bed under her bay window. Walter, though, who was inclined to worry, snored beside her. He was the only one who fit on her three-quarters bed.

A gibbous moon shone a silvery alien blue into the room. In his black mask and jumpsuit, Dick Bush pranced—silently as a cat—around Old Lady MacJenkins's chamber. He decided to get close to the bed to steal the platinum cross hanging over her headboard. Before reaching up to lift the crucifix, he looked through the items on her nightstand, where he found a book about herbal compound extraction and a journal. He placed the items in his sack.

Turning from the nightstand toward the bed, he saw Walter, with his droopy ears and nervous eyes, gazing right at him. The stealer stood still, smiled at the dog, and slowly reached inside his right pocket for his butterfly knife. But the traitor's hand didn't make it to the weapon before the saggy-faced dog decided to sound the alarm. . . .

Of course, as Sheriff Wineland says, it's hard to charge an old lady with murder, especially if she slept through the whole incident. All that she found in the morning, after she rose and looked out her window to check the weather, was a pile of bones, ripped-up clothing, that knife, and that knapsack. The good pets had even lapped up that robber's blood.

Eating Dick Bush aside, her dogs were a loving and playful bunch of giants. When she hosted the bridge club, each animal had its own card table to nap under. The ladies would often keep their feet warm by resting them on the beasts' massive heads and bodies.

BUT MRS. MACJENKINS WAS MORE than the keeper of giants. She was also the holder of a large tract of property in the Concord Pass. She had inherited the Pass from her father, along with her house in town, and had a large cabin out there where she spent her summers. From there, her runners could traffic moonshine up through the Pass into West Virginia.

Though her town house was the model of Southern Classicism—a brick house with Ionian columns supporting the roof of her front porch—her log cabin was a grand remnant of Concord's more rustic times. Outdoors she planted, in each corner, red cedars. Orange witch finger flowers grew over the house's walls and roof. Even the most discerning eye, looking up from Indian Pool below, could not distinguish her fortress from the forest.

Down the river from her, past the Pass, was Alistair's home—a perfect stone pentagon having a large front porch. The house sat on a hill rising from the floodplain, where the annual floods deposited a thin layer of silt. Radiating from the corners of his house, he planted mixed lines of pawpaw, persimmon, mayhaw, and mulberry trees. The tree crops also served as windbreaks, leaf-compost suppliers, and living fences for his five fields.

Every summer, Mrs. MacJenkins came to the river with her dogs and her grandson George, his parents having died a year after his birth, when they were swimming in Indian Pool and lightning struck the water. George often had his best friend Sammy Nolon out, and they'd swim in that same pool and climb the 150-foot walnut tree while she distilled liquor in the cabin. At night, mayflies flittered against the screens, trying to get inside as Mrs. MacJenkins, her grandson, and Sammy ate fresh bass and drank juice from Alistair's farm.

THEN, FOR WHATEVER REASON, SOMEONE in D.C. came up with the bright idea to build a dam at the end of the Pass. One day an urbanite official came knocking on Mrs. MacJenkins's front door in town and told her of the Government's plan.

"My land is not for sale," she stated.

"It doesn't much matter. The government has the right of eminent domain. That is—"

"But there's no just compensation; the Pass is priceless to me."

"The country needs power. The dam is an issue of federal security."

"I'll be an issue of federal security if you flood my front yard. Now get off of my property before I sic my dogs on you."

As she spoke, Otto, who was Frederick's grandfather, came to her side. He brushed his horse-sized head against her hip.

WHEN IT BECAME CLEAR THERE was little we could legally do to stop the Feds, we gathered at Alistair's pentagon farmhouse, out there below the Pass, to make defense plans. In his great dining room, we all sat down to eat.

The winter had passed and spring was just beginning. Yet still, Alistair had a rich store of sugary persimmons; delicate, chilled pawpaws; cinnamon medlars; mayhaw and mulberry jams; butternuts; and pecans to complement the big deer that Elise had caught with her dogs.

"It is a pleasure to have you all here at *Aurae Rustica*. I only wish that we could celebrate the start of spring under more relaxing circumstances. But we have some planning to do."

"I couldn't agree more, Alistair," Mrs. MacJenkins chimed in. "But first, if you don't mind, let's open this moonshine, which I have just concocted. I think it might inspire us."

THE FOLLOWING MAY, WHEN THE Army Corp of Engineers came to build the dam, they asked Alistair if he could provide them with drinking water from his well. No one else in town was willing to sell them a drop. He told them that his water was slightly tinged with clay and high in calcium, so it tasted hard, but would be fine. He stuck to a high price per gallon, and they took it.

THE TROOPS SET UP. MRS. MacJenkins moved out to her cabin for the summer, though she didn't make it to the river much. Every evening, the Indian woman named Flying Bird and her young daughter, Nancy, stood by the river, hurling spells at the troops.

The soldiers couldn't accomplish much. Shortly after their arrival, a strange delirium overcame them. At first they were plagued with dry mouths. They drank Alistair's water more feverously. Soon they were overcome with forgetfulness, unable to complete their tasks. The supervisors didn't know what orders to give. Mrs. Evangeline Rayburn commented that they seemed worse off than herself, and she was senile—or at least she thought she was.

After a few more days, their pupils began to dilate, making

the sun appear even brighter. Their lungs expanded, the extra air filling them with energy. Excited, they started swinging their tools at each other and giggling chronically. In the hot afternoon, the men began to skinny-dip and jump wholeheartedly into the river from the rope swing tied to the walnut tree in Mrs. MacJenkins's front yard. A week and a half after their arrival, they were all spending their days swimming and petting each other among the giant limestones.

As night came, they'd frolic back to the camp, where they devoured dinner, decorated their bodies with mud, and reveled around the campfire. Flying Bird and Nancy set up a tent nearby and taught them night dances. Often, Alistair would join the festivities. And as they partied, Tom Dorian led a team of townies to the construction site and undid whatever the soldiers had accomplished.

After a couple of weeks, a supervisor from D.C. came down to check on the progress. He nearly ruined his britches when he saw they'd accomplished nothing. He scolded the managers. But shortly after lunch, the phantastica infected him. Later that week he jumped, naked, from the great walnut tree's branches into Indian Pool.

THE SECRET, OF COURSE, WAS in the drinking water. For the new moonshine that Mrs. MacJenkins had opened at Alistair's dinner was almost indistinguishable from fresh water. It contained a little alcohol, but it also held the psychedelic compounds from jimsonweed and morning glory. The guests at Alistair's wowed in amazement when after one glass, large colors gushed into the room. It was then, laughing and hallucinating, that Elise MacJenkins revealed her plan to save the Pass.

Once while the troops were stationed here, someone nearly caught her. In mid-July, Tom's truck had a bad tire. So, Mrs. MacJenkins hauled the bottles of euphoric liquid over to Alistair's underground cistern, which was masquerading as a well. On her way over, a Federal pig—he actually looked like a pig—pulled her over for absolutely no reason.

"Ma'am, can I ask you why you have all those jugs in your backseat?"

"I get my water from Alistair MacGregor. I left something at his house while I was there, so I have to go back and pick it up."

"Are you sure that's water in there, ma'am?"

"Yes. Do you care to taste it?"

"For all I know, it's poison. I keep on telling Boss that something might be in the geezer's water, but he doesn't believe me."

"You haven't had any?"

"No, ma'am. I don't drink water. Fish fuck in it. I only drink milk."

"Really?"

"Yep. You can't go wrong with something that comes out of a tit."

"Alistair has the best water in the state. I drink it because it is high in calcium, so it's good for my bones."

"Then you won't mind if I ask you to down some right now. Afterwards, I'll be able to see if it affects your driving ability."

Mrs. MacJenkins stared at the cop.

"The road to Alistair MacGregor's runs along the Pass. Too bad there isn't a guardrail." He smirked.

Mrs. MacJenkins rose from her car, grabbed a jug, opened it, and turned it upside down over her head. With skill that would have impressed even William Carlisle, the town drunk, she downed the liquid for six solid seconds.

"Happy?" she asked, handing him the bottle. He took a few sips and shoved it back to her.

"I'll be happy when I see you drive through the Pass. Be careful not to go too slow. I'd hate to have a reason to think you were drunk."

Fortunately, over the years, Mrs. MacJenkins had done quite a lot of her own taste testing; she'd developed a tolerance about as high as a blue whale's. She had also outdriven a few men of the law in her bootlegging days. The pig, on the other hand, was not so learned. As he tried to keep up with Mrs. MacJenkins around Hairpin Curve, he lost control of his car. We often wonder what colors he saw as he fell, hundreds of feet, and crashed with a big boom on the dam project.

Years swam by. So many years passed that even a spiritual man of the Earth and a timeless woman of culture began to feel age in their joints. Mrs. MacJenkins's grandson George had gone off to Korea. She went to church every day, praying that he'd make it home. Often Alistair's daughter, Margaret, whom he had had very late in life, joined her. The river changed but did not tire.

THEN ELISE MACJENKINS'S GRANDSON RETURNED. When he arrived at the rail station, emancipated but amnesic concerning the war, his first question was how Flying Bird's daughter, Nancy, was doing.

He and Nancy had had a romance in high school. But the strain of his grandmother's disapproval of human hybridization had caused them to break up shortly before Korea. He had dated Margaret for a few months before heading off.

Upon coming back, though, he just wanted to see that Indian. "Nancy saves my soul," he told his grandmother.

"The first time I saw Flying Bird and Nancy, they only had feathers covering their twats," Mrs. MacJenkins snapped at George. He had come into her workroom to ask her blessing. She did not even look up from her still as she uttered her verdict. "A squaw—I'm sorry, but I can't."

HIS TEASED FLAME, MARGARET, MARRIED a local boy named Fit Hattanger. He was nice, but he was dumb and lacked the ability to speak plain English. "I understand the Greek better than that man," Mrs. MacJenkins pouted.

Moonshine.
Time.
Distillation.
Forgetfulness.

MRS. MACJENKINS WENT ON WITH her life. She had stored up a great deal of gold. She had her big dogs. She had her bridge and garden club parties. She had gossip and moonshine cocktails to share.

AND IT WAS EARLY SPRING, for the serviceberries were in bloom, when another hoity-toity came knocking on her door.

"Ma'am, I represent Virginia Energy. We want to build a massive hydroelectric dam at the end of the Concord Pass. Someone has bought the MacGregor farm and plans on turning it into a large development. This area needs power."

"I am sure Alistair is not willing to sell."

"His daughter has already signed the papers."

"But Alistair—"

"Is a very old man."

"Well, those people are going to have to retrieve power from somewhere else. My property is not for sale."

"There is an oil shortage, Mrs. MacJenkins. The local officials think this will do great things for Concord."

"IT WAS ALL FIT," ALISTAIR rumbled as Elise stood by his bed. "He's a stupid hick."

"Yes, I know. But how did this happen?"

"I've been signing property over to Margaret for years to avoid a death tax. I didn't think she'd listen to that redneck."

EVERYONE WHO WAS ANYONE SHOWED up to the meeting where the County Board of Supervisors were to approve the developer's plans to rezone Alistair's farm. Three minutes before the meeting was to start, the Ancients rode into the room. Clutching his walnut scythe, Alistair was on Onyx, who was the size of a bear. Elise sat sidesaddle on Frederick. Alistair wore a three-piece off-white linen suit, and Elise was in an off-white linen gown. Their long silvery hair streamed behind them. As they entered, Simon Donald and Ms. Tzigane yielded their seats to them in the front row.

Several people voiced their concerns about the dam. No one was for it. Sammy Nolon talked about how fish stocks in the river were going to be devastated. Betty Joe said we were going to flood some fine hunting woods. Ms. Tzigane informed everyone that there were an awful lot of brand-new cars in the board members' driveways. Steve Pampas rose up and called the entire board a bunch of morons.

The board thanked everyone for speaking and was about to vote, when Elise MacJenkins stood up.

"May I say something?"

The members looked at her with an uneasiness which they tried to mask with grins.

"I want to first apologize for my lack of eloquence. I am hardly a trained orator."

The board nodded to her, and she went on.

"Now, Alistair and I were almost late to this meeting because on our way here, we and a handful of other people got stuck behind a big old truck. At first, seeing the long line of automobiles in front of us, I thought we were going to a funeral. But when we realized that it was Tom Dorian's truck, we didn't mind the wait. Besides, we love that road to town.

"You have, in this room, men and women whose folks have been in Concord County for so long that they are intertwined in its history. Sitting behind me, you can see Carson Falkland, whose family founded the town, and whose great-grandfather, grandfather, and father all served as mayors. You have Betty Joe Lee deButt Carlisle, who is a descendant of General Lee. And, of course, there is Alistair—and me.

"For all of Concord's time, people have been enjoying the Fork River and the Pass. Carson's grandfather himself, so many years ago, told me his family believed the area was a great place for a town because the beautiful river had navigable waters. Why, Betty Joe, have I ever told you that Robert used to ride Traveller down the cliff-sided road? He would often stop at the spring near my father's cabin and water his horse. Sometimes he'd even take off his boots, walk down to the river, and wade around.

"The moment he died in his living room, water poured from the sky. When the river flooded, the coffin mill, up past my father's cabin, washed away. We sent some boys downriver to look for a box to bury our General in. However, I was the one who found the coffin, dangling in Methuselah's branches.

"When I think of Lee, I also think of the servants my father used to have around his cabin. My father was strict, but if they were good, he'd let them off early some afternoons, and they'd go swim in the river. I'd join them, even though I wasn't supposed to. During those moments—when the yellow sun sent warm beams down through the mountains, over the waving water and into us all—even field hands smiled.

"I met my first love in the Pass. He was a farmer, and I was somewhat older than he; we spent an entire summer swimming and playing among the rocks. We got into a fight at the end of that season; we did not want to change with the weather. We both went off and married other people. And though we have never been lovers, there are still evenings when I smile at how beautiful it was to be by the river and wrapped in the arms of a strong man.

"Lately, I've been thinking of my grandson. I've been remembering when he was a little boy, and like his father before him, I'd help him collect baby frogs along the river, and we'd sit with them jumping all around us on the water's edge. I think of his parents, who died shocked in an embrace in that water. I bear in mind his late wife, Nancy, whom I'm sorry I never saw swim with my grandson in the river. When I picture her and her mother, Flying Bird, I think of all the mistakes that we, as Southerners, make. I still remember my daddy's slaves. Then I smile, cry, and I mourn over my younger days."

For the only time anyone could remember, Mrs. MacJenkins

was crying, the years running down the map of her timeworn face.

"Gentlemen, please do not drown the walnut tree in front of my father's cabin. Every time I look at it, I see my boys."

MRS. MACJENKINS SAT DOWN, AND Frederick put his big head on her lap.

"All in favor of the dam, say 'Aye,'" spoke the Chairman, fat and red-faced.

All the board members said Aye.

"I guess I was headed to a funeral," Mrs. MacJenkins snuffled. She tapped Frederick gently on the head and then pointed to the Chairman of the Board.

Like a winged griffin, the dog jumped nine feet up and over the Board's table, sinking his teeth into the Chairman's neck. It snapped. Following Frederick's flight, Onyx came bellowing onto the oak table, taking another member by the face and ripping his head off. Simon Donald ran to the door and opened it up, letting Captain, Whitey, and Walter into the room to join the rebellion. One Board member whipped out a gun and was about to shoot Frederick, but Captain flew like a supercharged magnet to him. The leopard-shepherd snapped his jaws so tightly on his wrist that the man dropped his gun and screamed a bloodcurdling cry—heard by a tourist down the street. Captain held on; Onyx and Whitey grabbed the remaining supervisors and kept them hostage. Then Frederick, in a slow, gentle, humane manner, came to each living official. One by one, he grabbed them by the neck, giving each a quick life-ending crunch and yank.

Fit made a run for it, but Walter caught him by the britches on his way out the door. Frederick was about to put an end to him when Old Lady MacJenkins snapped her fingers. He halted.

Alistair hobbled up to the white trash, glaring at him. Margaret, crying, obediently stood by her father.

As if he were hitting a perfectly placed baseball, Alistair swung his scythe. The silver blade made a beautiful, new-moon shimmer as it flashed through the air, sunk perfectly into Fit's left ear, and then poked out of the right.

SHE DECLARED THAT WE'D FLOOD the pass over her dead body, and she meant it. When the Feds arrived to her cabin to haul her away, her dogs gave no sign of cooperating. They shot Frederick in the foyer, right as he ripped off a man's arm; Captain, on the stairs, as he tore out another man's Adam's apple; Whitey, in the upstairs hallway, after he darted out of a spare room and neutered a sergeant. They couldn't open her bedroom door, for Onyx leaned against it. After shooting through it, they still had a hard time pushing aside the bear-beast.

When they opened her chamber, she was sitting up in bed beside a dying Alistair, Walter dutifully at the end. She held a flintlock pistol from the Revolutionary War in her lap.

Sheriff Wineland, with tears in his eyes, stepped forward. "Elise. Alistair. It is time to leave."

"The Hell it is, Wineland," she thundered, cocking her flintlock and pointing it at him. "You'll have to blow me to pieces to drag me out of here. But if you do, let me warn you. Let me warn you all: My wrinkled map face will haunt you for the rest of your days. I've been part of Concord and the Fork River for a long time. My soul is rooted here enough to stick around a few extra seasons. So go ahead, old friend, shoot me. We're sticking it out."

Sheriff Wineland stepped back; the Feds didn't know what to do. They were filled with a stupor, as if they'd been inebriated by one of Mrs. MacJenkins's magical concoctions.

"Now leave me to mourn over Concord, Virginia."

WHEN THE FLOOD ARRIVED TO her great cabin, it was not like the one discussed in Genesis; this water did not fall from the sky. It was slow and creeping, inching its way, a surface like a plate of glass—suffocating the river's changes.

The water immortalized them. Simon Donald, looking through his telescope from the top of Deadman Mountain, reported that she and Alistair emerged from her cabin as the river started to claim Methuselah, the black walnut tree. She helped him as they scaled the nailed-on ladder planks, slowly making their way to the highest branches. There, high above Indian Pool, they rested, prayed to God, then pulled up the rope swing with their feeble hands.

They jumped, sailing through the air like a pendulum, releasing themselves at the most distant and highest point. Arms opening like the wings of a dove while holding each other's hands, the Ancients then, for old times' sake, gave that wild river one last dive.

If it form the one landscape that we the inconstant ones
Are constantly homesick for, this is chiefly
Because it dissolves in water . . .

Having nothing to hide. Dear, I know nothing of
Either, but when I try to imagine a faultless love
Or the life to come, what I hear is the murmur
Of underground streams, what I see is a limestone landscape.

—W. H. Auden, *In Praise of Limestone*

ACKNOWLEDGMENTS

Special thanks to (in random order)

Angelo Verga and the Cornelia Street Café
Earl Dax, curator/impresario, scenedowntown.com
Casey McLain
Leslie Strongwater and Dixon Place Theater
Jason Eagan and Ars Nova Theater
Richard Gottlieb
TC Rice and Christy Park
Cynthia Rosenzweig and the CCSR at NASA/GISS
The Pirate's Alley William Faulkner Society, especially Rosemary James and Michael Murphy
My editor at St. Martin's Press

And the supportive audiences who saw these stories in performance and provided constructive feedback and inspiration. Family members making trips to NYC from Virginia and West Virginia; friends I thought I might not see again; famous environmental scientists; classmates from college or high school, traveling from as far away as California; individuals I met on the subway or at a party; aspiring writers and artists, as well as luminaries; and the spirits of those who are still with us.

I feel so fortunate to have so many wonderful people in *Concord, Virginia.*

NOTES

28 Kinkead, E. *In Every War But One.*
31 Luke 10:19
31 Mark 16:17–18
34 John 1:1
36 Psalm 40:1–3
36 Psalm 40:5–6
37 John 1:3
38 Psalm 40:8–9
38 John 1:5
38 Genesis 1:12
39 Psalm 40:10
40 John 1:17
40 Psalm 40:11
40 Genesis 1:20
44 Psalm 40:12–14
46 Genesis 1:1
46 John 1:1
47 Psalm 14:1
47 Psalm 40:15–17
47 Quetzalcoatl 111, trans. John Bierhorst
66 Adapted from a tale told by Mack C. Ford to Zora Neale Hurston, *Every Tongue Got to Confess: Negro Folk-tales from the Gulf States.*
72 Adapted from a tale told by Lily May Beale to Zora Neale Hurston, *Every Tongue Got to Confess: Negro Folk-tales from the Gulf States.*
111 Adapted from the sworn statement of Private John Shaw before

South Carolina's governor on August 21, 1754. Reprinted in Fred Anderson's *Crucible of War.*

142 Adapted from a story told to Tihomir Djordjevic by a Yugoslavian Gypsy nailmaker in Aleksinac and translated into English by Fanny Foster in 1936. Reprinted in Diane Tong's *Gypsy Folk Tales.*

SELECTED BIBLIOGRAPHY

Listed below are some of the works that informed and inspired this text.

Aeschylus. *Prometheus Bound*. Trans. Henry D. Thoreau.

Anderson, Fred. *Crucible of War.*

Audubon Society. *Field Guide to Birds.*

Bierhorst, John (ed.). *In the Trail of the Wind.*

———. *Four Masterworks of American Indian Literature.*

Burstein, Andrew. *Jefferson's Secrets.*

Carlson, Lewis H. *Remembered Prisoners of a Forgotten War* (with interviews from, among others, Robert A. MacLean, Larry Zellers, Harly Coon, James Dick, Glenn Reynolds, Jack Browning, Irv Langell, William H. Funchess).

Coffee, David W. "Thomas Jefferson, Patrick Henry, and the Natural Bridge of Virginia."

Crawford, Alan Pell. *Twilight at Monticello.*

Dunn, Susan. *Dominion of Memories.*

Goldstein, Donald M., and Harry J. Maihafer. *The Korean War.*

Granfield, Linda. *I Remember Korea.*

Harwood, Doug. *The Rockbridge Advocate.*

Howard, John. *Men Like That.*

Hurston, Zora Neale. *Every Tongue Got to Confess.*

Jabbar, Kareem Abdul. *Brothers in Arms.*

Jellis, Rosemary. *Bird Sounds and Their Meaning.*

Jurinek, Jerilyn. *American History Paintings.*

Katz, Jonathan. *Gay American History.*

Kluger, Richard. *Simple Justice.*